Jemima: A Prickle Creek Romance

ANNIE SEATON

Home to the Outback: Book 3

This book is a work of fiction. Names, characters, places, magazines and incidents are the product of the author's imagination or are used fictitiously. Any resemblance to actual events, locales, or persons, living or dead, is coincidental.

Previously published in the US as His Outback Nanny (2017)

ISBN 978-1-7638747-9-4

Home to the Outback series
Prickle Creek romances

1. Lucy
2. Angie
3. Jemima
4. Isabella

Prologue

Jemima Smythe ignored her ringing phone as the stylist touched up the last of her make-up. She sat straight, the clinging blue silk of the formal evening dress whispering against her bare legs. The fashion parade was at the Sydney Opera House, and everyone was on their best behaviour. This was her chance to get to New York. She'd heard there was a talent scout from the Eileen Ford agency in the crowd today. The problem was that everyone else was excited, but Jemima wasn't. Lately, she'd been a bit bored by it all, though the prestige of getting picked up by the New York agency kept her going. Not to mention the financial benefit—she'd be set for life, and *then* she could do what she really wanted.

'You're next up, darling,' Roger called. Next on the catwalk, and if she answered this call, she'd miss her cue, and Roger, the volatile stage manager, would go berserk. Usually, Jemima worked on being serene and presenting a calm exterior to the world. It was amazing how many favours—and indeed extra jobs—she'd picked up because of her reputation as an easy-to-get-on-with model, not a prima donna, no matter how hard the shoot or the day on the catwalk was.

Sometimes, she wondered if she had chosen the right

career. The hard work and the long hours didn't faze her. It was attitude that was important. This was a short-term job, and Jemima knew she'd been very lucky. Hard work and the right attitude *had* paid off. Many of the younger models seemed to believe that a career in modelling was a path to fame and riches. But she'd been luckier than most. She'd started modelling for a department store in Sydney straight after high school, and by the ripe old age of twenty-five, she had saved a lot of money and made some shrewd investments. More often than not, Jemima found herself mentoring the young girls aspiring for a quick path to the top. She shook her head, and the stylist grunted.

'Sorry.'

But despite the "glamorous" perception of her job, it *was* difficult work, and it was lonely work. On the road most of the time, following the fashion circuit, she missed the quiet life of Prickle Creek, where she'd grown up. No one needed her here. If she disappeared, she'd be replaced by the next new "face." It was all so shallow, so artificial—but it paid the bills . . . and more.

The stylist put his make-up brush down. 'You're right to go. Perfect, as usual. And listen, the word is the guy from New York is in the front row. Kill 'em, babe.'

Jemima glanced down at her phone, and all serenity fled. A familiar number flashed onto the screen.

Oh, bloody hell, why is Gran calling?

Not now. She had to be calm. This was her chance to hit the big time.

***

One month later

Jemima pulled out into the heavy Sydney traffic on the motorway to the west, her Audi sports car making a muted roar. For some reason, she always felt as though she had to impress her big brother, Liam, and he'd certainly been impressed with her new car when she'd picked him up from the international airport. He'd looked tired and had quickly fallen asleep. When he'd woken up, and she'd turned onto the Golden Highway, he'd been ready to chat, and they'd talked nonstop as they headed for Dubbo. She was still finding it hard to believe that they had both dropped everything and headed home to the outback at Gran's request.

'The accident really changed our lives, didn't it? I think of everything as before and after,' Jemima said with a sigh as the golden fields of wheat flashed past.

'Me, too.' Liam slowed again as they came up behind a cattle truck, and the smell of cattle seeped through the vents. 'At this rate, we won't be there until almost dark. But it'll be good to be home for a while.'

'You still think of it as home? Funny. So do I,' Jemima said.

They were quiet for a while as Liam concentrated on the road, each lost in their own thoughts.

Jemima took in a deep breath. 'Ah, the smell of the country. I've missed it.'

'Have you been out here lately?'

'No.' She shook her head. 'This is the first time since the funeral, and I'm a bit nervous.'

'Don't worry. You're not Robinson Crusoe.'

Three hours later, Jemima cursed and fought for control as the Audi slipped from left to right on the wet road. A light shower had turned the six-kilometre stretch of dirt road between the main Prickle Creek Road and Prickle Creek Farm into a slippery track. It took them more than half an hour to get to the gate of the property, and when the red and green sign appeared on the fence, she pulled over. 'I'd forgotten how far down the road the farm was. But it still looks the same, doesn't it?'

'It does. I feel about eighteen again. PRICKLE CREEK FARM,' Liam read the words on the sign before he turned to her. 'Why did you stop?'

'Because I need confidence and war paint.'

He huffed an impatient sigh when she reached for the make-up bag on the floor of the back seat and proceeded to make up her face before brushing her long hair and putting it up with a clip. She finished off with bright red lipstick and a light spray of perfume.

'Gawd, Jemmy. I'll stink, too. Give it a break.'

'Jemima and it's Chanel No 5.' She looked at him as she

started the car again.

Liam shook his head. 'Do women really think that stuff makes a man look twice?'

'Oh, button it, Liam.' Jemima took a deep breath. 'If you want the truth, I'm nervous as hell about going home. I can hide behind it. Jemima Smythe, the aloof model who doesn't do emotion.'

Liam grinned at her. 'Well, if you did, I think your face would crack with all that gunk on it.'

For that, he copped a punch on his upper arm.

'We're not all as confident as you are. And don't you even think about saying a word of that to Gran or Lucy,' Jemima said.

'Don't worry, sis. We're all in this together. Solidarity. Okay?'

Despite his teasing, Jemima knew her brother was also nervous about coming home. Why had they all jumped to Gran's summons so readily? From all over the world? Maybe it was because she'd never asked them for anything before.

Maybe it was because they wanted a new start in life.

'Solidarity,' she murmured quietly.

Chapter One

Twelve months later

Jemima Smythe's gaze was fixed on the red, dusty road as she walked down the long driveway to the mailbox. It was mid-January, and the brown snakes were active out here at Gran and Pop's farm in the Pilliga Scrub, but Jemima couldn't go off into a daydream. Keeping an eye out for movement in the tall grass on the side of the driveway was a must if you walked along the road in summer.

The sun was bright, and Jemima squinted as she opened the flap on the mailbox and pulled out the Prickle Creek Farm mailbag. There was a sheaf of letters, advertising brochures, and the local weekly paper. She took the newspaper and slipped it beneath her arm as she flipped through the letters.

It seemed almost a lifetime ago since she had received that phone call from Gran. After she'd collected Liam from the international airport in Sydney, they'd come home, and Gran revealed that she wanted each of them to spend some time at Prickle Creek Farm. Her grandparents were considering selling the farm, but they wanted to give the grandchildren a chance to work it and see if any of their futures were here in the Pilliga Scrub. For eight months, Jemima had fulfilled her contractual obligations in

New York at the Eileen Ford Agency, but her heart hadn't been in it. She'd been home now for a couple of months, helping Liam—Gran and Pop had toured the UK and now were on a bus trip through Europe—and Jemima was ready to start a new job—doing something she wanted to do, something that was worthwhile and she enjoyed.

Yes!

There was a letter in an official-looking envelope—from the school. Her hands were shaking, and Jemima opened it, her eyes scanning the words. She let out a loud whoop, startling a murder of crows high up in the trees above the gate. They flew away with a couple of loud and cranky *ark ark* calls.

She read the letter aloud as she walked along. Reading out loud made it seem so much more real.

'Dear Ms Smythe, please report to Prickle Creek School office at 8.30 a.m. on Monday 29th January to be interviewed for the position of kindergarten teacher.'

Yes! She had an interview! The first step towards getting her dream job was underway. Lucy had asked her about it when she'd come over with baby James a couple of days ago.

'Jemmy, I can't understand you. You had a job that many girls dream about. You've got enough money saved to live off for years, a snazzy little sports car, and yet you want to go and work in a primary school?' Lucy had screwed her nose up in disgust or confusion. Jemima hadn't been sure which.

'I do. It will be so satisfying. I'll be making a difference. Helping the children to learn. Teaching them to grow into responsible citizens. In my hometown.'

Lucy had shaken her head. 'And wiping runny noses, and putting Band-Aids on cut knees, separating fighting children. Not for me.'

'You've got your own little boy to love.' Jemima's voice was soft. 'I want someone to need me, Luce.'

Lucy had married Garth McKenzie from the farm next door, and their baby, James, was now three months old.

Lucy reached out and squeezed her hand. 'I'm sorry, love. I'm so happy. I get caught up in my little world with Garth and James; I don't think of others. I so hope it works out for you.'

'Oh, Lucy. I'm going to love it. It means so much more to me than being a clotheshorse. Going from city to city, having make-up plastered all over my face became so hard towards the end. I hated it. Even in New York, where everyone wants to work. I'm so happy to be home in Prickle Creek. But I need to make my own way and find somewhere else to live.'

'What did Liam say about you teaching?'

To everyone's astonishment, once his six months had been up, Liam had decided to stay at the farm. He was also involved with an alliance that was fighting the introduction of coal seam gas and doing some casual reporting for the local Prickle Creek paper. Liam had also reunited with his former lover, Angie, the local veterinarian in town.

Jemima was now living with Liam, and he'd done nothing but complain about her cooking since she arrived.

'I haven't told him or Angie yet. I didn't want to jinx my chances by telling too many others. But you know, that's the reason I need to do something. I'm happy for them, but I feel like a third wheel here. Once their house is built, it'll be better, but I know when they head off into town some nights, it's because they want some privacy. Once I get the job at the school—and I'm trying to be positive—I'll find somewhere to live in town.' She giggled. 'Liam certainly won't miss my cooking.'

'That's for sure, love.' Lucy laughed along with her. 'You certainly missed out on Gran's cooking gene.'

When Jemima was almost back to the farmhouse, she glanced at the newspaper and her buoyant mood deflated in an instant.

'Oh, no.' She groaned as she read the lead article on the front page. Who the heck talked to the paper?

As she scanned the text below, her mood worsened. Not only was the content incorrect, but they also spelled her name wrong.

Jennina Smythe! She walked heavily up the front steps as

she read. *From the New York Catwalk to the Country.*

Everyone in Prickle Creek would know her business by nightfall. *Just what I don't need.* She hoped the principal of the primary school didn't read the paper this week.

###

Liam didn't look impressed when Jemima fronted him with the newspaper as soon as he walked in from the paddock.

'Are you responsible for this?' She knew her voice was shrill, but damn it, she was still angry.

He raised his hands and stared back at her. 'At least let a man have a shower and clean up before you're into him. And I have no idea what you're on about.'

'This.' She shook the paper at him, and he took it from her. He held it up and read the headline, and a smile tipped her brother's lips. At least Jemima was sure she saw one before he answered.

'Don't go blaming me. I didn't tell them a thing.'

'You work there.' Her voice was full of accusation.

'I am a casual journalist on staff, submitting *occasional* political articles about coal seam gas mining in the district. Why the heck would I want to write an article about you?' Liam chuckled and held up the paper. 'And the proof is there. I think I can spell my little sister's name properly.'

'I'm cross.' Jemima pouted.

'I can see that.' Liam crossed to the window and looked up the driveway. 'I hope Garth and Lucy aren't too much longer. I'm starving.'

Jemima went into the kitchen, turned the oven on for the pizzas, and bit her lip. She was still angry about the stupid article. She opened the dresser and took out a tablecloth, ready to set the table.

'So, what's so bad about being in the local paper?' Liam asked.

'I was going to tell you tonight when Lucy and Garth were here, but I might as well tell you now.'

'So, spill,' Liam said with a curious glance at her.

'I've got a job interview.' Jemima shook the tablecloth and spread it over the old wooden table in the centre of the kitchen. 'The farm's under control. You and Angie need some space. You've hired a cook to look after the contractors this year, which means I'm certainly not needed here.'

'Where's the job? Back in Sydney?' Liam asked.

'No. At the primary school in town.'

'You finished your teaching degree?' Liam ran his hand through his hair.

'I did. And now I'm worried about this stupid article.' Jemima crossed to the sink. She watched as Garth drove through the gate and brought the SUV to a stop. Lucy spotted her at the window and waved.

'Why?' Liam frowned. 'Surely that won't affect your chances of getting the job?'

'I guess it's a confidence thing. I wanted to slip into the school quietly, get the job and just be Miss Smythe, the new teacher.' She held out her hand for the newspaper, and Liam passed it back to her, and she read it again. 'What credibility is a "famous international catwalk glider"'—she shuddered—' going to have in the classroom or with the parents at Prickle Creek Public School?'

'You're a local girl made good, Jem. The kids—and parents—will love you.'

She grimaced. 'I am. This is where I grew up, and this is where I want to be. But the first step is getting the job before I can show them anything. And *then* I can focus on showing them I'm a hometown girl.'

'So I wonder who gave the information to the local paper?' Liam crossed to the door and held it open for Garth as he came in loaded with pizzas on one arm and a drinks cooler in the other. Lucy was close behind him, with baby James on her hip. 'It wasn't me.'

'I saw the front page of the paper when I was in town this morning,' Lucy said. 'Everyone was talking about it in the grocery store. I was surprised to see it, Jemmy.' Lucy put the baby on the soft rug on the floor, and he gurgled contentedly. 'Did the paper interview you?'

'No. I've got no idea who gave all that guff to the paper. A catwalk *glider*, for goodness' sake!' Jemima shook her head. 'And listen to this. They make me sound as though I've been living the high life. "New York, Monte Carlo, Paris—our local town has a celebrity in its midst." And I've never even been to Paris!'

Lucy walked over to the oven. 'So, who else knew you were in the fashion industry?'

'One of the librarians at the town library asked me what I'd done in Sydney the other day, but—'

'Well, there's your answer then. Maisey Sykes is the biggest gossip in town.' Lucy unwrapped the pizzas that Garth had carried in and put them into the large gas oven.

'I suppose it'll be a ten-minute wonder, but I so wish it hadn't been before my interview on Monday.'

'Oh, cool! You got an interview?' Lucy walked over and hugged Jemima as the guys headed out to the verandah. 'You'll be fine, Jemmy—a whole new career for you. I'm so happy you've moved back home for good. All we need now is for Seb to return— and stay!'

'Whoever would have thought?' Jemima smiled and nodded to the driveway. 'Speaking of love, here's Angie.' They both watched as Liam hurried out to greet her. He swooped her in a hug, and Lucy smiled. 'Ain't love grand!'

'If that's what you want out of life.' Jemima kept her voice light; just because her love life was non-existent didn't mean she couldn't be happy for her brother.

Lucy pulled a bottle of champagne from the cooler that Garth had carried in as Liam held the screen door open for Angie. 'Hi Angie. Perfect timing. Let's toast to a new career. Miss Smythe, soon-to-be the best school teacher in Prickle Creek. Good luck, Jemmy!'

Jemima and Lucy giggled at the surprised look on Angie's face.

Chapter Two

Ned McCormack tripped over the two school bags, sitting plumb bang in the middle of the hallway as he raced towards the kitchen. The smell of burning toast filled the old farmhouse, and smoke billowed from the toaster to the ceiling. Four-year-old Ryan was sitting at the table, banging his car on the tabletop. Next to him, an iPad was churning out nursery rhymes at full volume.

'Kelsey? Gwennie? Who's watching the toast?' Ned yelled as he stopped at the kitchen door. As he spoke, the smoke alarm in the kitchen came on, and the high-pitched squealing covered his son's muffled reply.

'What?' Ned grabbed a tea towel and flicked it at the alarm until it finally stopped.

Ryan stopped banging his car on the table just long enough to answer his father. 'Kelsey put the toast in, and then she ran outside. 'Cause Gwennie's in the shed, and she screamed for us to come see.'

'God, what now? Come see what?' Although Ned was well used to his drama queen daughter and her screams.

'Rosie's got her kittens.' Bang, bang, bang.

Ned took a deep breath and crossed to the back door. He

stood and concentrated on keeping his voice pleasant as he called across the yard. 'Kelsey, Gwennie. Come and have breakfast, please. You've got ten minutes before I'm driving you to school.'

There was no way he could let them catch the school bus on their first day at a new school. Even though Kelsey had stood there last night, hands on hip—just like Cathy used to stand—and insisted that she could look after Gwennie. Even though it meant he had to drive into town twice today, the afternoon trip to town was the important one. The appointment with the bank manager was crucial. And that's what had been doing his head in.

He had to hire some help so he could balance his time on the farm with the time he spent with the kids. Otherwise, there was no point in them living out here. The problem was there wasn't enough money left to hire a farm worker. Ned did not doubt that he could manage repayments on a loan, and the upside would be a better family life, but he had to get it first.

At least he could get the grocery shopping out of the way after he drove them to school.

As the girls came into the kitchen, Ned pulled the pieces of blackened toast from the toaster and put them in the overflowing kitchen bin. 'Where's the bread?'

'That was the last two slices.' Kelsey opened the fridge. 'And there's no milk to have with cereal.'

'There's long-life milk in the cupboard, Kelsey.' Ned

smiled, and his voice was patient. 'For when we run out, remember.'

Kelsey rolled her eyes. 'What about bread?'

'There's bread in the freezer.' Ned was pretty chuffed he had this grocery shopping thing under control.

Ryan's big brown eyes—pansy eyes the same as his mother's—widened and then filled with tears. 'But I want eggs.'

'You girls, go and get dressed. Your new school uniforms are hanging up in the laundry. I'll cook some scrambled eggs for all of us, and then we'll get you to school. I'm sure it won't matter if we're a bit late.'

The two smiles that lit up the kitchen added to his certainty that he'd made the right decision to move out here.

'You'll bring us in to our new school?' Gwennie's voice wobbled.

'I will, and you'll love it. It's where I went to school.'

'I wonder if I'll have the same kinder teacher as you?'

Ned smiled as he ruffled Gwennie's hair. 'I don't think so, chicken. I'm sure Mrs McGillicuddy was a hundred when she taught me.'

'Me, too?' Ryan cried out. 'I want school, too!'

'Preschool for you when we get settled, buddy. But how about a milkshake after we do the shopping?'

'No fair.' Kelsey stamped her foot. 'We have to go to a new

school, and he gets a milkshake!'

Kelsey could be difficult when she thought things weren't going her way.

'I'm sure you had many milkshakes before you started school.'

'I did. With Mum.' Her voice was quiet as she stared past him.

'Yes.' Ned turned away and looked out at the paddocks when the girls disappeared into the laundry to get their uniforms. 'You did,' he said quietly.

With Cath.

Ryan resumed the car banging. Ned gritted his teeth inside the smile he forced to his face.

By the time he drove into Prickle Creek, dropped the girls off, did the grocery shopping, went to Cartwright's produce store, and then drove back out to the farm, the best part of the working day would be gone. At least he could pick up the salt blocks and get them out into the paddocks before he had to turn around and go back into town, pick up the girls, and then get to the bank at three o'clock.

Kelsey skipped down the hall, and as he opened the fridge to get the eggs out—luckily, the hens had performed well yesterday—a little hand tugged on his T-shirt. He looked down to see Gwennie's wide eyes staring up at him. She was a perceptive little soul, and she knew what he was thinking.

'It's okay, Daddy. I'll put the groceries away this afternoon while you feed the cattle. We can mind Ryan, and then Kelsey and I will get tea ready. We can have salad so we won't burn anything.'

Always the carer, his little Gwennie.

The last four years had been a nightmare, and he'd tried to do the best he could for his three kids. Moving to the country and back to the family farm had been an attempt to get them away from the memories and make a new start as a family. A new start, although in a place that was familiar to him. Even though it needed a huge amount of work—and money—to make it a going concern, the farm was the place where he'd grown up—before marriage and kids and before the sad times when his life had been turned upside down in one single day.

'I'll do you a deal.' He crouched down in front of his youngest daughter. 'You can help Kelsey make the salad, and I'll cook some sausages on the barbie. What do you think about that?'

Gwennie sounded happier as she put her arms around his neck. 'That sounds just perfect. I do love you, Daddy.'

'I love you, too, bub.'

A wet kiss landed on his cheek, and Gwennie let go of him and scurried down the hallway.

##

Ryan chatted all the way into town, but the two girls were

quiet. It was the second time they'd changed schools in the last year—when the house had been sold; they'd all moved in with Cath's parents for three months until Ned had finished the contracted work at the construction firm in Sydney. But if he could make the farm profitable, they'd be at Prickle Creek Public School for a long time.

The problem was that Kelsey was in Year Six, and she had her heart set on going to boarding school the next year. She was horse-mad, and she'd found a school in Armidale—the result of a Google search—that had a strong equestrian program. When she'd shown him the website, Ned had hidden the groan. He didn't want Kelsey to go away; he wanted his kids close so he could keep them safe.

'We'll see, love,' he'd said. 'Who knows? You might find the local high school has a good program, too. Besides, it's still a year away.'

Ned focused on the road ahead as the list of his chores filled his thoughts. Once he dropped the girls at the school, he'd make a quick trip to the produce store and then do the grocery shopping. Ryan loved the trip up and down the grocery aisles, although the small co-op grocery store in Prickle Creek was nothing like the bright, noisy, and busy shopping plazas they were used to on the north shore of Sydney. He'd checked the working account before he'd left home: there was just enough there to get the salt blocks he needed and do a medium-sized grocery shop.

Doubt settled in Ned's chest as he wondered for the umpteenth time whether he'd made the right decision for the kids and their future. Since Cath had died, he and the kids had struggled along as best they could as he'd continued his job in the city in Sydney. The night that he'd come home—after an hour's drive in heavy traffic to Dee Why on the northern beaches—to discover that the babysitter had left early and eleven-year-old Kelsey was in charge—was the day he'd known they couldn't go on like that. He'd put the house on the market, and it had sold the first day. He'd given notice at his job as a construction manager at the big city firm where he was overseeing the redevelopment of an inner-city shopping mall and had made plans to move back home to the Pilliga Scrub.

The family farm was in need of attention. It had been overseen by a succession of managers since Mum and Dad had retired to the coast, and Dad hadn't replaced the last guy when he'd left. Dad had sold off the cattle and let the wheat fields lie fallow. He'd often talked about selling the property but hadn't been able to bring himself to put it on the market.

After moving in with Cath's parents while he'd worked out his contract and squirrelled away every cent he could, they'd spent Christmas at the beach with his parents. The kids had been so excited as they'd packed up at the end of the short holiday, ready to head to the farm on Boxing Day. It had buoyed up Ned's spirits to see their excitement. He'd been a bit down since he'd finally given away Cath's clothes to the op shop before they'd moved in with her parents.

A new start. A new life.

Now, he was determined to ensure his kids were happy and financially secure.

Chapter Three

Ned let out a sigh of relief as he glanced at his watch as the small township came into view. Then past the vet surgery, past Cartwright's produce store, through Main Street, past the IGA grocery store, past the historical museum on the corner, across the bridge over the river-with-no-water and then into the car park at the side of the school. They'd made it before nine o'clock; the school buses were still dropping children off at the front of the school.

Children and parents milled around the front of the school, and he smiled. It was very different to the SUVs and lycra-clad-on-the-way-to-the-gym mothers of the Sydney north shore. Here, there was a queue of dusty farm utes with hay bales in the back and lots of checked shirts and jeans. Satisfaction filled him. He'd come home to his place, and although it was the last thing he'd expected, it felt right.

Before Ned could open his door, the two girls were out of the car, in their nicely pressed uniforms and their new school bags on their backs. He'd learned a lot of new skills over the past four years. He climbed out of the car, opened the back door, and cupped his hand on Ryan's cheek. 'Come on, buddy. Wake up. We're here.'

Kelsey and Gwennie were waiting on the footpath, holding hands.

'You girls got your lunch boxes?'

They both nodded, and Ned's eyes narrowed at Kelsey's innocent expression.

'Take the iPad out of your bag and put it in the car, Kelsey.'

'X-ray vision, Daddy?' she asked but laughed and did as she was told.

'Good try. Superhero Dad, remember.'

Kelsey and Gwennie walked ahead of him, still holding hands, and he held onto Ryan as they made their way to the front office of the school. The office was a hive of activity as students ran in and out. Half a dozen parents stood at the counter waiting to be attended to, and telephones rang incessantly.

'Come on, kids. We'll sit down and wait our turn.' He led them over to the three spare seats by the door and they sat down, Ryan sitting on Ned's knee as they waited for the girls to be allocated to their classes. He'd completed the enrolment procedure before they'd left Sydney. Ned had wanted to be sure that Prickle Creek was suitable for his girls but it seemed not a lot had changed since he'd gone there. A good solid country school where the students were taught well.

The crowd cleared slowly, and as it was almost their turn,

Gwennie grabbed his arm. 'Daddy, I think I'm going to throw up.'

He stood and put Ryan on the chair. 'Kelsey, look after your brother.' He grabbed Gwennie's hand and hurried across to the office window, interrupting the woman who was speaking on the phone. 'Where's the ladies' restroom, please?'

She pointed to a half-open door next to the office that was marked "Principal" in gold letters. They hurried across the foyer, Gwennie's hand over her mouth, and Ned pushed the door open. There was a corridor ahead with a photocopying room, a couple of small offices, a storeroom, and a restroom at the far end. The toilet door was open, and Gwennie pushed past him, ran up the hall, and shut the door.

All was quiet. Ned leaned against the door and sighed.

Gwennie put on such a tough front, but neither of the girls had got over Cath's death.

Of course, they hadn't.

This morning was the first time Ned had mentioned her name for weeks. The grief counsellor had said to talk about Cath a lot to help the girls cope, but as the four years had passed, it had been too hard. Moving to the farm was a new start, and Ned was determined to make it work. If mentioning Cath naturally was going to help, he would do it. There were many changes to be made, and the meeting at the bank this afternoon was crucial to his success.

As Ned waited, a door opened along the corridor, and he glanced up. A woman in a red tailored suit stepped out and walked towards him. She was tall—almost as tall as he was, and he was just over six foot. Her fair hair was scraped back into a severe bun, and her face was pale, but her deep blue eyes held his as he stepped back to let her pass.

'Daddy, quick.' Gwennie's cry was followed by the sound of her throwing up.

The tall woman stopped and frowned. 'Do you need some help here?' she asked kindly.

Ned had been about to open the door and then paused when he remembered it was the rest room for the female staff. He looked at the woman and his mouth dropped open.

Jemima? Jemima Smythe? Liam's little sister?

'Jemima?' he asked hesitantly. 'Are you the school principal?'

Piercing blue eyes stared back at him without recognition. 'Yes, I'm Jemima, but I'm not the principal.'

'Can you go in and help Gwennie for me? Or at least check the coast is clear and I can go in and look after her.'

'I'd be happy to.' She shot him a curious look as she pushed open the door. 'Mr…?'

'McCormack. Ned McCormack. I was Liam's friend at school.'

Her eyes widened, but she didn't say anything before she went into the restroom and the door closed behind her. He put his ear to the door trying to hear if Gwennie was okay, but all he could hear was Jemima's soft voice.

He hadn't caught up with Liam yet, but it looked like his baby sister was a teacher at the school they'd all attended when they were kids.

But Jemima wasn't a child any more. She'd always been a tall girl when she'd traipsed around behind Liam and him when they'd been in high school. But she'd sure grown into those long legs. She was drop-dead freakin' beautiful.

The door opened, and Gwennie came out, wiping her hands on the side of her shorts. Her face was clean, and he looked over her head at Jemima.

'She's fine now. Just nerves, I think. We've washed her face, and she said she's okay.'

'Yep, I'm okay now, Daddy.'

'Thank you, Jemima, or should I say Miss Smythe, or is it Mrs these days?' Ned didn't want it to sound like he was fishing to see if she was single. 'I mean, what do the children call you?'

'Jemima is fine,' she said as she looked nervously over her shoulder. 'I'm in a bit of a hurry. Um, nice to see you, Ned.'

Ned watched as she hurried down the hall and disappeared through the door into the foyer. She moved elegantly, and her skirt and jacket moulded drop-dead gorgeous curves.

He swallowed as Gwennie tugged at his hand. 'Come on, Daddy. Let's get this over with.'

By the time the girls were placed in their classes and given a buddy to take them to class, Gwennie looked a bit happier, and Ned put Ryan back into the car and headed for the grocery store.

'Come on, buddy. Let's go get a milkshake.'

This would work. Ned loved his kids and wanted them to be happy. That was more important than anything, and this was the place to make sure it happened.

Chapter Four

After her interview at the school, Jemima couldn't settle. She had her mobile phone in her pocket. Mrs Sykes, the principal—what were the chances of a connection with the librarian, she wondered—had said that they would notify the successful applicant this afternoon, with a view to starting by the end of the week. But more than that, she couldn't get Ned McCormack out of her mind.

Fancy running into Ned. Obviously married, with a daughter, and living in Prickle Creek. He'd been a looker when he was in high school, but he'd grown into a fine-looking man. Tall and broad-shouldered, and still with those gorgeous eyes and cheekbones. She wondered which local girl he'd married.

Jemima had brought a change of clothes to town and called in at Angie's house to get changed. Angie hadn't gone to work yet. She and Liam had come back into town last night. Angie held up a coffee mug as Jemima came through from the bathroom in her jeans and checked shirt.

'Yes, please. Love one.'

'How did it go, Jemmy?'

'Good, I think. The questions were easy, but it's a long time since I've done a job interview. The principal was friendly enough, and she told me all about the school and let me ask a lot of questions.' She squeezed her hands in front of her. 'Anyway, I'll know later today. I'm going to stay in town until I hear. If I'm successful, I can go to the school and get organised. Fingers crossed, anyway.'

'Make yourself at home here. There's not many places to fill in a day in Prickle Creek.'

Jemima took the coffee that Angie passed over and cupped her hands around the mug. 'Thank you. Gosh, I'm so nervous. Would you believe I was more nervous about this interview than I was before any of the big fashion shows in New York? After I came out, still shaking, I bumped into one of the school dads—an old friend of Liam's— and I was so worked up after the interview I could barely string a sentence together. He probably thought I was rude.'

'I'm sure he didn't.' Angie laughed. 'I can understand why you were nervous. It's because you want it so badly.' She shook her head. 'Are you sure you really want to be a teacher? It's such a different life to what you're used to.'

'I'm sure. It's wonderful to be back home.' Jemima grinned at Angie. 'Except for having to live with my brother until you marry him. 'Are *you* really sure that's what you want?' she teased.

'Point taken.' Angie grinned back at her. 'We all know

what we want out of life. Or we think we do.'

Jemima stood and rinsed her coffee cup on the sink. 'While I think of it, do you know if there's a connection between Mrs. Sykes in the library and the school principal?'

Angie nodded. 'Yes. They're sisters-in-law. And there's another Mrs. Sykes, too. She works at the bank. The three brothers apparently moved to town a few years ago and bought up a lot of land around the district.'

'Oh, gosh. I do hope the library one hasn't gossiped to the principal about my past career. I didn't mention it. I didn't think it was relevant.'

'It's nothing to be ashamed of, Jemmy, and it has nothing to do with whether you are suitable for the job. You made a success of what you did and studied at the same time, and that's pretty impressive.'

'Thanks, Ange. Anyway, fingers crossed. And fingers crossed that she hasn't read the paper yet.'

'Let me know when you hear.'

***

The call came at two-thirty when Jemima was sitting in the milk bar, having her third coffee. She'd already toured the museum, learned all about the local bushrangers—it would be a good place to bring a class to learn about Australian history—called in at the library, done the grocery shopping, and snagged a table at the milk bar while she waited. She sat and stared at the main street; not much had changed since she'd left home. The shop fronts still needed a coat of paint, and a couple of the smaller stores had FOR LEASE signs in their windows. It was sad to see Prickle Creek losing its vibrancy.

She jumped and grabbed for her phone as it buzzed on the table.

Disappointment settled in her chest like a stone as Mrs. Sykes advised she hadn't gotten the job. The successful applicant was a new graduate from the same university where Jemima had completed her course.

'Thank you for letting me know.' Jemima stared across the road as she held the phone to her ear. She'd remain professional, even though the let-down cut like a knife.

'Mrs Sykes, is there any feedback you can give me? About my interview technique. How I could improve my answers?'

'Your answers were fine. The teacher the panel chose was from a small town, and we felt that *her* background aligned more closely with our school goals. Don't be too disappointed. With your background, I'm sure there'll be plenty of other opportunities for you.'

'My background?'

'Working internationally. Your skill set will open up many jobs for you.'

Not in Prickle Creek, thought Jemima

'Thank you for the opportunity of being interviewed.' She put her phone down and bit her lip, trying to overcome the disappointment that was coursing through her. She *was* a small-town girl, and this was where she wanted to be. Teaching came naturally to her, and she loved being with children. How could she get that across and remove that image of her that everyone here seemed to have? She silently cursed that newspaper article and then realised that a positive approach was what she needed.

Jemima headed to the newsagent's store, purpose in her step. There was no point being down about it. If she couldn't teach at the school, there were plenty of other opportunities to implement her teaching skills. She purchased a packet of square, lined cards and a black pen and walked to the library. When she'd been there earlier in the day, she'd seen a community notice board filled with cards for all sorts of **FOR SALES, POSITIONS VACANT,** and **WORK WANTED** ads. She sat at a table in the library and drafted an advertisement. It took three cards before she was happy.

Qualified teacher available as a nanny/governess. Prepared to live-in if required. Willing to teach/care for any age child.

She added her number to the bottom of the card and walked across to the community notice board. There were spare pins along the bottom, and Jemima crouched down to pull one out. As she pinned the card to the centre of the board, she felt a tug on the bottom of her shirt. She glanced down and smiled. It was Gwennie, the young student she'd helped this morning.

'Hello,' the little girl said shyly.

'Hello again. Did you have a good day, Gwennie? No more feeling sick?'

'I was better, and I did, and I made lots of friends, and I learned lots, too.'

'What have you got there?'

Gwennie frowned and held out a card. 'I can't reach and if I put it on the bottom no one grown up will see it. Would you please pin mine up high?'

'Sure.' Jemima took the card, and as she went to pin it up, she read it and hesitated.

Oh dear.

She crouched down beside the small girl. 'Gwennie,' she said, 'I can't put that on the board for you.'

Small white teeth bit trembling lips, as Gwennie looked at Jemima. 'Did I make a mistake with my words?'

'No, sweetie, it's all good, but does anyone know you're putting that ad up?'

'No, I wanted it to be a surprise for Daddy when I found us a new Mummy.'

Jemima read the card again and her heart went out to this

little girl. 'A new Mummy?' She wondered where Ned's wife was.

'Maybe we should ask Daddy for the best phone number to put on it. You did forget to add one.'

'Oh, silly me.' Gwennie let out a very grown-up sigh. 'I guess we'll have to ask Daddy then, because I don't even know the name of the road our new farm is on. It's only new to us though, it's old for Daddy.'

'Where is Daddy?' Jemima looked around but the only other people in sight were the sour Maisey Sykes and an elderly woman checking out a book.

'He's up the road at the bank. I'm supposed to be waiting with Ryan and Kelsey but I sneaked out when Kelsey wasn't watching.' She let out another sad sigh and Jemima's heart almost broke. 'But I guess Daddy will have to know now because I do need a phone number, don't I?'

Jemima held out her hand, trying not to think of this little girl running across the main street where the cattle and wheat trucks constantly sped through town. 'How about I walk you across the road and take you back to the bank?'

Gwennie would be lucky to be seven-years-old. *What is Ned thinking leaving her in the supervision of another child?*

She looked at Jemima and nodded. 'That would be very kind of you.'

As they turned, Gwennie looked up at the board. 'What's

your ad for?' She stood on her tippy toes and read the words on Jemima's card slowly and her precise pronunciation was perfect.

'Oh wow!' Her cute little face lit up in a huge grin. 'That's perfect! Take it down right now.'

Jemima tipped her head to the side and smiled. 'But I've only just put it up.'

'Oh please, please take it down. You don't need to. You can be our new mummy.' She held up her card. 'Then I won't have to advertise, after all.'

'Come on, we'll go and see your daddy first.'

Gwennie put her hand in Jemima's, and as they headed out of the library to the main street, she chattered away.

'My sister's name is Kelsey, and she loves horses, but she likes the new kittens, too. Ryan is a cry-baby, but he's still only a little, and we don't have a dog yet. Well, we have an old working dog, but I'm not allowed to play with him. Daddy isn't sure if he's been vass- vassin—'

'Vaccinated?'

'Yes, that's it. Daddy said he doesn't want us to get those worms.

Jemima shivered. 'Where do you live?' Then she remembered that Gwennie hadn't known the name of the road their farm was on. 'Sorry, I forgot you didn't know.'

Gwennie nodded. 'It's not like Sydney, where I could read

all the street signs. And you know, I think we're going to get on just fine. You can help with our homework, too, seeing you are a gover—govern— '

'Governess.' Jemima said distractedly. It was unfair to ask Gwennie too many questions. She wished she knew what had happened before she took Gwennie back to Ned. But it wasn't the right thing to ask a little girl who was advertising for a new mother.

She'd have a quiet word with Ned about what his daughter was up to.

Jemima held her hand firmly as they stood at the side of the road. A road train came thundering into town, and she smiled as Gwennie covered her nose with her free hand.

'Oh, dear. I forgot to ask you,' she said with a worried frown. 'If you're going to come and be our new mummy, you'll have to like the smell of cattle because we live on a farm. Is that all right?'

Once they'd reached the other side of the street and stood outside the bank, Gwennie tugged her hand.

'I hope Daddy won't be cross with me.' Her little voice was quiet. 'I only did it because I heard him on the phone to Grandpa the other night, and he said he needs to spend more time out on the farm, but with Ryan and us girls, he hasn't got enough time. Since Mummy went to heaven, Daddy has looked after us all by his self.'

Jemima's heart contracted, and her eyes stung as she looked into the earnest face of the little girl.

'Come on. Let's take you back to Daddy. He used to be best friends with my brother a long time ago when I was a little girl just like you. I'm sure he won't be cross.'

Chapter Five

Ned shook Paul Crowe's hand and ignored the despair that was gripping his chest. For a second, he worried he was having a heart attack. He couldn't do that. The kids wouldn't have anyone. He took a deep breath and the tightness eased.

It was stress, pure and simple.

'I'm sorry I can't be more positive, Ned, but without a proven record on the land, I can't authorise a rural loan. If it was for something other than wages, I could perhaps use it as security, but just to hire a worker or two? Sorry.' The bank manager looked sombre. 'I know it's not a good option, but I can approve a credit card that will give you enough credit to see you through the year.'

They crossed the office to the door, and Ned shook his head. 'Not at thirty percent interest. Thanks, Paul.'

He pushed open the door, and Paul walked out with him.

Gwennie ran across the waiting area. 'Daddy, Daddy. Look who's here!'

He lifted his head and stared. It was Jemima, but she no longer wore the red suit. Instead, a loose checked shirt hung open over a white T-shirt and a pair of slim-fitting jeans. Her long legs—and boy, were they long—ended in a pair of dusty work boots. She smiled at him, and he tried to smile back.

Gwennie tugged at his hand, and Ned was lost for words when she pulled him over to her.

'Our new mummy's here.'

Before Ned could speak, Paul strode past him and held out his hand to Jemima. 'Well, let me be the first to congratulate you, Jemima.' Paul turned to Ned as he shook her hand. 'You old son of a gun, if you'd mentioned that you were marrying Jemima, there would have been no problem with the loan approval.'

Luckily for Ned's sanity, Ryan dropped the new car that Ned had bought at the supermarket this morning and began to bellow. 'Now it's broked. Kelsey, you broked it. You broked it, you broked it. I want a new one.'

The bank teller was staring at them, with her mouth open. Jemima held Ned's eye as he crossed to the chair and lifted Ryan off Kelsey's lap. As he stared back at her, she shook her head slightly in an almost imperceptible movement, and he swallowed down the denial that hovered.

'Ned, I've got another appointment now, but give me a call later. The loan won't be a problem. Don't worry about coming into town until I call you to sign the papers.' Paul patted his shoulder as Ned's hands were busy trying to stop Ryan from crawling down his body to the floor.

Ned nodded and waited until the door to the bank

manager's office closed.

'What was all that about?' he said in a cracked voice. He cleared his throat and put Ryan down on the floor.

'Hello again, Ned.' She nodded, and a sweet smile crossed her face. She lowered her voice to a whisper as Gwennie sat down on the floor next to Ryan. 'I need to have a quick word with you about Gwennie. Have you got time to come and have a coffee?'

'And maybe you can tell me why Paul Crowe instantly approved a loan when he thought you were my—um—fiancée.' He scratched his head as she nodded. 'Come on, kids. Milkshake time.' Ned took Ryan's hand and followed Jemima out of the bank.

At the back of the milk bar there were a couple of old pinball machines—Ned was sure they were the same ones that had been there when he'd been in high school. He watched as Kelsey and Gwennie each held one of Ryan's hands and led him to the games.

He shook his head and leaned back in his chair.

'Country banks. It's a bit more informal than I'm used to.'

Jemima was sitting opposite him at the table. They'd ordered coffee and were waiting for the kids' milkshakes.

Ned ran his hand through his hair.

'What a day. I guess there's some sort of apology in order, too. What did Gwennie do?'

Jemima shook her head. 'Don't worry about it. No harm

done. I just wanted to make sure she got back safely. You've got your hands full, Ned.'

He sighed and ran his hand over the stubble on his chin. He must look like a derro. He and Ryan had ended up in the hay shed after he'd got home with the groceries, and he hadn't left enough time to shave or get changed before he'd rushed back into town. No wonder Paul had knocked back his loan application.

Until he thought he was engaged to Jemima.

Bloody hell. What is going on?

'No, tell me. I need to know what she'd been up to. She's a sweet kid, but she can be a loose cannon sometimes. I could tell you some stories.'

'She was putting an ad up on the library noticeboard for a new mummy.'

'Oh God.' Ned put a hand over his eyes for a moment. He dropped it and shook his head again. 'So, tell me how you applied and were selected so quickly.' He tried to smile to lighten the moment, but he was sure it came out as a grimace. 'I'm sorry. A very serious talk with young Miss Gwennie will be first priority when we get home.'

'Please, there's no need to apologise.' Jemima put her hand out and touched his, and he looked down at her long fingers as they lightly brushed his hand. Her nails were short and square, coloured with some sort of pale pink polish. 'I'm sorry for your loss, Ned.'

'Thanks, Jemmy. Do you still answer to that?'

Her smile was wide, and again, Ned was taken aback by her beauty. Jemima's skin was flawless, her blue eyes wide and clear surrounded by thick dark lashes and brows that contrasted with her blond hair. She'd changed from the gangly little girl with braids that he remembered teasing when he'd been at their house all those years ago.

'Recently, I have been. Since I came home. I'm with Liam at Gran and Pop's place, across the road from your gate.'

'Liam's back in the Pilliga, too? Fantastic. I haven't caught up with anyone much since I've been back. I've been too busy. Last I heard, he was a reporter in London.'

'He came back last year. We all did. Or almost all. Sebastian will be back soon, too…do you remember Lucy and Seb? Our cousins? Maybe you won't remember Seb; he's younger than I am.'

'A vague memory. And you're working at the local school now?' Ned glanced to the back of the shop. Con, the milk bar owner, had delivered the milkshakes to the kids, and they were sitting quietly drinking them.

'No, I was just there for an interview. But it didn't work out.'

'Sorry to hear that. You know, I remember being envious of Liam and his extended family. I only had one sister, and Jenny's a lot older than me. She'd already married and left the farm before I'd even started high school.

'You have a beautiful little family of your own now,' Jemmy said, looking at the children.

Ned's heart swelled with pride. 'I do.'

Jemmy leaned forward and touched his hand again. 'Ned, I don't want to pry, but I think I can help you out. Please tell me if I'm overstepping the mark.'

He held her steady gaze and nodded. 'What do you mean?'

'I guess you were going for a loan and got knocked back?'

'I did. I need to hire a farmhand or two on the property. It's mine now.' He gave a mirthless laugh as he looked at her. Jemima's wide eyes were fixed on his, and Ned found it hard to look away. Her expression was full of understanding. 'I never wanted to work on the farm. When Dad retired to the coast, he took on a few managers, but they never worked out. So when I was looking for a way to be able to look after the kids and still have an income, the farm was the answer. I bought out my sister's share.'

He spread his hands open on the table. 'So now, I'm home in Prickle Creek. The last place I ever thought I'd come back to. And I'm already wondering if I've made a mistake.'

'A mistake?'

'Yes. I'm finding it impossible to balance the farm work with looking after the kids. Thus, the visit to the bank today to get some help.' Ned frowned. 'But why did Paul change his mind when he heard what Gwennie said? I don't want to sound rude, but how does you being "their new Mummy" make such a difference in getting a loan?'

'Ned?' Jemima reached out and took his hand, and her fingers tightened on his. 'I have a suggestion for you.'

Her lips were set in a straight line, and there was no sign of a smile anymore. Her beautiful high-arched eyebrows lowered in a frown, and two cute wrinkles appeared between them. 'Listen carefully, and don't answer until you hear me out. Maybe this suggestion can help both of us. I'm looking for a job—but not because I need the money.'

He frowned and opened his mouth to speak, but she put her other hand up.

'Hear me out first. Like I said, I had an interview for a teaching position. I'm a qualified teacher, but I didn't get the job.' She leaned forward in the chair, and he caught a whiff of a subtle, but sweet floral perfume. 'You need someone to help you with the children, right? So you can work on the farm?'

He nodded.

'If you had more time, would you still need the loan to hire some more workers?'

He looked down at her hand, grasping his fingers, and a long-forgotten quiver tingled up his arm. 'Yes. I need more than one set of hands to get the property up and running.'

'If I help you out, I'll be accepted as a local, and I know that will help me get a teaching job here. When they're at school'—she looked over at Ryan— 'I guess the little one is still home?'

'Yes.'

Someone to mind the children while he worked on the farm. That would make such a difference, but Ned lifted his hand away and shook his head.

'I'm sorry, Jemima. I can't afford a nanny, too. I'd love to help you out, but—'

'No. Listen to me. I don't want to get paid. I don't *need* to get paid. And if it helps you get the loan if I pretend to be your fiancée'—her voice wasn't as confident now, and Ned had to lean forward to hear what she had to say— 'it helps us both out.'

***

Jemima sat back and took a deep breath. Ned was looking at her, and she couldn't read his expression. Her heart was thudding, and she wondered what the heck she'd just suggested.

'You've lost me. Why would being your . . .fiancé guarantee me a loan on the spot? And why would you want to come and work for someone with three kids for no pay? Especially if you're looking for a paid teaching job?' He scratched his head. When he'd hung out with Liam, Jemima had been too young to tag along, and she hadn't taken any notice of her brother's best mate.

Ned had been a tall, skinny teenager, and now he had filled out and grown into his height. He was a broad-shouldered man with a strong face. He had the most gorgeous cheekbones and was as good-looking as any of the male models that she'd worked with over the years. His hair was dark and in need of a trim. He looked tired, and she guessed the shadows beneath his eyes were from late nights while he tried to be both mother and father, as well as run a farm and worry about finances. She didn't think she'd seen him smile yet, but even with his serious expression, he was a good-looking man. A shimmy of warmth settled in her tummy as he held her gaze, and she pulled a face. 'I guess you haven't read the local paper this week then.'

He shook his head. 'No. I was going to buy it on the way home.'

She pushed her chair back and went over to the rack where the café owner provided newspapers and magazines for the customers. The local paper was on top, and she gulped as she looked at the photo that took up three-quarters of the front page. It was the last fashion show she'd done at the Sydney Opera House. At least it was a decent photo. She picked it up, took it across to the table, and put it in front of Ned.

'My life in one photo and a paragraph. You can read it. I hate talking about myself. But please take it with a grain of salt.

It's exaggerated, and I suspect that report had a bit to do with me not getting the job at the school.'

Ned scanned the paper, and Jemima smiled up at Con as he put their coffee on the table. She pulled out a twenty-dollar note and paid for the coffee and milkshakes as Ned read.

'Wow, New York,' he said when he finally looked up and put the paper on the table. 'You've got a great job. Or you *had* a great job. But you said you've moved back to the farm?'

'No.' She shook her head. 'No, it wasn't "wow," I mean. Hard work in an artificial world. But it *did* leave me comfortable financially.'

'So why did you come back to Prickle Creek?'

'Last summer, Pop had a knee operation. Gran called us all home to take a turn on the farm to see if we wanted to keep it in the family.'

'And?'

'We all came home and did our stint, except for Sebastian. He says he's coming, but I'll believe it when he actually arrives. Liam and Lucy have settled here to stay, but I'll let Liam catch you up on that. If I can get a job here—doing what I love—I'll stay, too. I did my teaching degree while I was working and travelling. And being home near family is important to me.'

'Family is the most important thing there is, and we often don't realise that until it's too late.' Ned's voice was low, and his eyes were bleak as they held hers. Jemima could almost feel his sadness. 'We need to talk about this. Are you sure—?'

'Ryan, stop it!' A loud cry came from the back of the shop, and Ryan ran down between the tables.

'Go home, Daddy?' The little boy tugged at Ned's hand to try to get him to stand up.

'In a little while. What have you been up to, you little larrikin? Tormenting your sisters again?' Ned picked him up onto his knee and held the little boy firm with one hand while he drank his coffee. 'Soon, mate.' He smiled at Jemima for the first time, and she was pleased to see the sadness disappear from his expression. It was hard to look away from those soulful dark eyes, but she forced herself to look down.

'Jemmy, it's not the right time to talk with these kids around. I'll certainly think about what you said, but I feel like I'd be taking advantage of you. If I do accept your kind offer, we'll come to some sort of arrangement.'

'Please think about it. I'm serious. And I'd love to help out.' Jemima pulled one of the blank cards from her bag and wrote her mobile number and the Prickle Creek Farm number on it. 'When you want to talk some more, give me a call.'

She stood, and Ned lifted Ryan off his lap. 'Go and tell your sisters it's time to go.

Ned took Jemima's hand. Butterflies fluttered in her

tummy, and she raised her eyes to meet his. He held her gaze for a long moment before he spoke. 'I'll give you a call in a day or two.'

Those butterflies went crazy as he kept hold of her hand until Gwennie pushed between them.

'Come on, Daddy.'

Even though she should be feeling upset about not getting the school job, Jemima couldn't help the smile that tugged at her lips as she walked back to the car.

Chapter Six

As Ned drove back out to the farm, an open-top silver sports car overtook them on a long, clear, straight; a wild tangle of blonde hair flying in the wind as the car zoomed past.

'Look, Daddy.' Gwennie's voice was a high-pitched squeal. 'It's our new mum.'

'Stop it, Gwennie,' Kelsey said curtly. 'You're being stupid. We haven't got a new mum. And we don't need one.'

Ned glanced back at the girls in the rear-vision mirror after the Audi TT had surged ahead of them. Kelsey's face was like thunder, and he swallowed. While Jemima's offer was generous and would certainly solve a lot of his problems, there was more to consider than bank loans, keeping the washing up to date and keeping the house in order. He had the kids to think about too. But if he didn't consider it, he wouldn't be able to afford the farm help, and they might not be able to stay.

He was caught between a rock and a hard place. It didn't matter that Jemmy was a Prickle Creek girl. Look at her now. She was an international model, for goodness' sake.

But while the three kids were all here in the car, and a captive audience—Kelsey was one to run away and hide when she didn't want to talk about something—it was probably a good time to broach it. He had to.

Softly, softly.

'Did you know that I've known Jemmy forever? Her brother and I were best friends. Their farm is just across from ours now. But they used to live in town, and when I was your age, I used to go there for sleepovers. Jemima was just a little girl then.'

'I forgot you went to school here.' Kelsey sat up, and Ned was pleased to see she looked a bit more interested.

'And you know what else I remember? Jemima used to be a champion rider at pony club.'

Now he had Kelsey's full interest. He felt a little bit dishonest playing the horse card, but if it was going to help…

'In Prickle Creek?' she asked.

'Yes, Liam said she was very good.'

'Does she still have horses?'

'I don't know. You'll have to ask her. I'll ask her to come over one afternoon. She's offered to give us a bit of a hand. Or better still, we could go over and visit their farm. I'd like to catch up with Liam.' Ned glanced in the mirror again. Suspicion warred with interest on Kelsey's face.

'Maybe we could. Do you think she probably does have a horse? Would she let me ride it?'

'Probably.' *In for a penny, in for a pound.* 'If we get Jemmy to come over and help with your schoolwork and babysit Ryan, I can do more work through the day. What would you think about that?'

Gwennie squealed, and Ned winced as her excited screams echoed around the car.

'That would be awesome, awesome sauce, Daddy.'

'Keep it quieter, Gwennie.'

'Yeah, put a lid on it, Gwennie. Daddy needs to think,' Kelsey added.

Ned smothered a smile when Kelsey nodded. She was a smart kid, and she knew that her chances of getting her own horse depended on him making a success of the farm.

'Sounds like a plan,' she said.

Ned was thoughtful as he turned onto the dirt road that led to their farms. One big advantage was that Prickle Creek Farm was only a kilometre or so from their front gate so Jemmy could come over with little notice if he did accept her offer.

All in all, maybe it hadn't been such a bad day.

***

After he waved the girls off on the school bus the next morning, Ned called Jemima's mobile.

'Hi, it's Ned. Are you free to come over this afternoon?'

'I am, what time?' she replied, and Ned smiled.

'About two.'

'Okay, sounds good. See you then.'

That would give them time to talk before the girls got home from school. Ned had lain awake most of the night doing the PMIs. That had been a Cath thing. She'd been so logical. Whenever they'd had a decision to make, she'd pull out a large piece of paper and draw three columns.

'PMI time,' she'd say, her brown eyes twinkling. The feeling that hit Ned as he thought about it was as real as a kick in the stomach.

Pluses, minuses, and interestings of Jemima's suggestion. What were they? The one he thought of last night had gone when he'd woken up this morning. He'd sit down before she came and make a list.

But as usual, Ned's plans for the day went awry. As soon as he waved the girls off on the bus—pleased to see they had already made some friends—he began to make his list and had started on the pluses when he remembered he had to get the washing on before it was too late to hang it out. The girls' school clothes from yesterday were still in the linen basket; they only had a couple of the blue school shirts each. When he went to put the first load of washing on, the washing machine groaned and came to a stop. There was no water coming into it, and the power cut when it tried to start the wash cycle with no water in the drum. Further investigation revealed that there was no water anywhere in the house, and he grabbed Ryan and drove down to the pump at the bore. Three hours later, they were still there. Luckily, he'd thought to throw a box of cars and a couple of apples in the ute when they'd left the house.

'Daddy? I'm starving.' Ryan's plaintive cry had Ned looking at his watch, and he blinked when he realised it was way past lunchtime. His phone had rung non-stop as he'd tried to work, and as he'd worried about the calls, he'd not focused on the task at hand. It was almost two o'clock. Jemmy would be arriving soon, and the house was in chaos. If he shut the doors, she wouldn't be able to see the unmade beds and most of the mess. He didn't want to frighten her off before they'd even discussed her idea.

'Sorry, mate. Just about fixed now. You've been a good helper.' Despite the fact that he'd achieved nothing he'd planned to do today, he couldn't help but grin when he looked at his boy. Just as well he'd finally fixed the pump because Ryan had been playing in the red dirt. He'd need a bath—and food— when they got back to the house.

As they drove towards the back gate of the house paddock, a puff of dust rising above the front gate indicated Jemima's arrival. Ned got out of the car, opened the gate to the house yard, drove through, and then got out again and closed it. It would be so much easier when Ryan was big enough to help him around the place.

Don't wish their lives away, Ned.

Cath's voice echoed through his head. He hadn't coped well with the kids when they were babies: the nappy changing, the night crying, and the sicking-up. Cath had gently chastised him once when he'd said he couldn't wait until Kelsey was a toddler. *Don't wish their lives away, darling.*

But when Ryan had been a baby, Cath had been in the hospital on life support, and then her injuries had taken her away from them. Ryan didn't remember her at all. He'd been too little.

Now Ned closed his eyes and clenched his jaw.

What am I going to do? What is the best thing to do for the kids?

***

Jemima pulled up at the front of the McCormack farmhouse. She'd never been down to the homestead before, but she'd driven past the farm gate many times. The McCormack farm was one of the first farms on the Come-by-Chance road, and the house looked as though it was still the original homestead. It was a square house with a gently sloping tin roof that then overhung the wide verandah in a gentle bullnose curve. The wrought iron lace that filled the corner was rusty and full of cobwebs—an old house, neglected for a long time, but full of promise. The driveway circled a centre garden edged with rocks, but the rose bushes were withered and brown, with only a few faded blooms hanging sadly from a couple of bushes at one end. Jemima loved being in a garden. Both she and Lucy had inherited the love-of-flowers gene from Gran, but lucky Lucy had also inherited Gran's cooking skills, which were sadly lacking from Jemima's repertoire.

She parked the car and took another good look at the house. The timber on the veranda floor was worn, and the paint was peeling on the eaves too. Ned had his work cut out for him here at the house as well as out on the farm. She'd noticed that a lot of the fence posts were rotten and the wire was hanging loose on a couple of the paddocks that fronted the main road.

Jemima opened the door and slowly got out of the car. Liam had taken the farm ute down to the back dam and was working on the pipes, so she'd had to bring her Audi. She felt self-conscious driving such an ostentatious sports car in the district. All it did was reinforce that stupid article in the local paper. When she got home, she was going to list it on Gumtree and buy a vehicle more suited to farm life. There was no need to add to the impression that she was some glamorous blow-in. She was a local again. She'd buy a small SUV more suitable for out here in the bush.

There was a dusty farm ute parked at the side of the house, so it looked as though Ned was there. Jemima swallowed and straightened her T-shirt. She had resisted her automatic instinct to dress up to come and meet with Ned. Casual and work-like jeans and a T-shirt would help her convince him that this was a good idea. For both of them. Plus, she didn't want it to look like she was trying to come onto him. She'd pushed away that warm feeling that had stayed with her after she'd driven away. It was the first time she'd felt that tug of attraction to a man for a long while. There were more important reasons to help out than the fact that he was a fine-looking man.

She'd given more thought to her idea, and the more she'd thought about it, the more attractive it was.

One: It would fill in her days.

Two: It would give Angie and Liam more privacy if she stayed over at Ned's place.

Three: It would show that she was staying and part of the town, *and* would prove to the school that she was a lot more than a retired fashion model.

Four and the reason that she knew was making her want this so much: Someone would *need* her. Jemima was a nurturer. That was the main motivation for her wanting to be a school teacher. Liam had Angie, Lucy had Garth and little James, Gran and Pop had each other, Sebastian—well, she didn't know about him, but he always seemed busy and happy.

She had no one. Jemima was lonely. Helping Ned would fill the void that she'd hoped the teaching job would have filled. This would be the same but on a smaller scale.

As far as Ned went, she was sure he would welcome her

with open arms. It would give him more time to work on the farm; it would—with some discussion—help him with his loan, and she could look after his little boy, do the house chores for him, do the laundry… And maybe he'd let her help out in that poor garden.

Five: There had been a spark between them, and she knew she would enjoy spending time in Ned's company. He was a good man.

A perfect solution for everyone. Surely Ned had come to that conclusion, too.

So, when Jemima tapped on the door, and a still serious-faced Ned answered, she was taken aback.

'*Ssh,*' he said without the glimmer of a smile. 'Ryan's asleep.' He gestured to the couch, and Jemima drew a surprised breath. The little boy was sound asleep and covered in red dust.

'He went to sleep in the ute on the way back from the bore, and I didn't have the heart to wake him. He hasn't even had his lunch yet.'

Her fingers itched to get a face washer and clean the little boy's face, but she fought it. Jemima kept her head high and ignored the chaos in the house as she walked through the living room. Or she tried to. It was hard to ignore the clothes and toys on the floor and the dirty dishes on every surface. Living alone for so long had made her pedantic about being tidy, and she was forever picking up after Liam at Gran's house and chastising him for being a slob.

But this? This mess was in a league of its own.

Straightening her shoulders, she followed Ned into the office adjacent to the kitchen, where he gestured politely to the chair beside the desk.

'Please sit down.' His voice was crisp and business-like.

Her stomach sank. It was going to be just like the job interview at the school where she'd been judged and found wanting.

She moved the breakfast cereal box from the spare seat and put it on the floor before she sat down. At least Ned had the grace to look embarrassed and moved it onto the desk.

'Sorry. One of Ryan's bad habits.' But still no welcoming smile.

This was a very different Ned from the one she'd had coffee with yesterday. Maybe without the children, he was more serious. Maybe he only put on the happy face when they were around. Jemima was confused, and her self-confidence fled.

He cleared his throat and lifted a piece of paper from the desk without meeting her eye. The happy anticipation that had filled her since she'd met Gwennie in the library yesterday trickled away.

'So, I've done an analysis of your proposition. A plus minus—'

'And interesting,' Jemima said. 'De Bono's theory.'

That got his attention. He lifted his head and met her eye. 'Um, is it? I'm not sure what it's called.'

Jemima lifted her chin a fraction higher. If he was going to be formal, she would, too. 'It is. Carry on.'

'Well, in terms of what you've suggested, the pluses certainly are a positive for my consideration.'

'That's good.'

'But in terms of benefits for you, there's really only the experience for your resume. I can't afford to pay you, and I wouldn't feel comfortable about that at all.'

Jemima leaned forward. 'Look, you need a loan. Apparently, you can't get one without me, and you need someone to watch your kids. I can provide the collateral, and I can help care for your kids. I get the experience I need, and you get a nanny. Win-win. It's not like I'm giving you the money'—she hurried to qualify her words—'and it's neighbourly. You need a hand. I'm free. And I'm more than happy to help you out.'

Ned brushed the back of his hand against his cheek. Jemima stared. Even though there was now a streak of red dust on one cheek, he was clean-shaven, and his hair was a bit tidier. Maybe he'd made an effort because she was coming over.

He was one fine-looking man. She shook herself and ignored the funny feeling in her chest. Nerves, that's all it was. She wanted to do this.

'I don't think I should take you up on your offer, however neighbourly.'

'Why not?' Cold disappointment replaced the warm feeling in her chest. She clenched her hands on her lap and looked down at them as he kept talking.

'Jemima, you're an international fashion model driving an Audi, for God's sake. How long will you be happy out in the bush, washing, cooking and cleaning, and helping my kids with their homework?'

She sat up straight, and her voice was cold. 'You disappoint me, Ned. You're the same as everyone else in this town, assuming that you know what I want.' She leaned forward. 'What I want is to live back here in the hometown that I love, have the job that I want to do—be a teacher, like I've wanted to ever since I finished high school.' She held out her hand to him and then pulled it back and put it in her lap. 'This is the perfect opportunity for me to be seen as a member of this community, which *I* know I already am. I just need to convince the community that I'm serious about living here and starting a new career. Working here with your kids will prove that I'm serious about teaching. I won't give up. I'm here to stay.'

He took a breath, and Jemima held hers as he looked at her for a long moment. 'You really mean that?' he said.

'Of course I do.' She lowered her voice, and this time, she reached out and put her hand on his arm. 'Ned, it's what I want. And you can help me get it.'

'Okay. You've been more than honest with me. This is my dilemma. If I don't get the loan, I can't hire farm help, and we can't stay here on the farm for much longer. Like you, I want to stay. I want to bring my kids up out here and spend time with them.' He cleared his throat. 'So, the benefit for me is we can stay here. I guess it sounds the same for you. The one thing that really bothers me is how casual it will be, so I have a condition.'

She looked up. His shoulders were square, and his face was unsmiling. Jemima realised he was as nervous as she was.

'A condition?' she parroted.

'I've made a few calls today. There are two things. First, to ensure that the bank accepts the collateral you put up for the loan, we need to formalise things.'

'With a signed contract? I suppose if you think that's necessary.'

'No. By getting married.'

'What?' Jemima gawped at Ned. *What did he say?* 'Did you say, "get married"?'

'I did.' He ran his hand through his hair, and it stood up in tufts. If it hadn't been Ned McCormack sitting across from her, Jemima would have felt it was a bit creepy. But it was Ned, and she was sure he had a good reason for saying what he had.

'Okay, so . . . Paul Crowe rang from the bank. There are two ways we can do this. As well as giving me gushing congratulations about "hooking the catch of the town"—'

'Seriously? How sexist is that!' Jemima stared at Ned. 'What else did he say?'

Ned fiddled with the pen on his desk. 'He outlined the financial obligations of the rural loan. As my fiancée, you can provide collateral for my loan by going guarantor. The problem there is, if I don't make a go of this, and I go broke, you're responsible. You would have to pay the loan back out of *your* money.'

Jemima nodded slowly. 'Not a good option. We both know how uncertain the land can be.'

Ned sighed, and Jemima felt sorry for him.

'No, I couldn't risk that,' he said. 'But I've talked to a few more people today.'

Jemima frowned. It was okay to be seen as helping out with the kids' schoolwork, but she didn't want the whole town to know that she was helping Ned out financially.

'Don't worry, I didn't call anyone local. I talked to the head of the branch bank in Sydney—I didn't want Paul to get wind of any more questions and there is another option. To ensure that the bank accepts the collateral you put up for the loan, the only way you're not liable for any default on the loan is if we formalise our relationship.'

'By getting married?' Jemima stared at Ned. 'That's the only way?'

'Yes.' He took a deep breath and held her eyes with his. 'I didn't mean to blurt it out like that. Sorry. He said if we're married—he asked my intentions about dates, but I fobbed him off—the loan is approved automatically without the risk of you losing any money. It sounds crazy, but that's the way the rural co-op banks work.'

'Old-fashioned standards, I guess,' Jemima said. 'Different to the city banks.'

'Very.' Ned looked glum.

'You said there were two things,' she asked as she tried to process what he'd outlined.

'Yes. I've taken some more calls this afternoon. I'd forgotten what Prickle Creek was like. Very different to the anonymous life you can lead in the city.'

'What sort of calls?'

He rolled his eyes. 'Two Sykes' calls. Maisey Sykes from the library called to tell me what a wonderful mother you'll make for the children and how lovely you and Gwennie looked together yesterday. And asking whether the girls were going to be bridesmaids!'

Jemima knew she was gawking. 'Oh, my goodness.'

'Then Mrs Sykes, the school principal, rang, saying how wonderful it was that the children would have a mother now and did I think you would help out at the school. Maybe volunteer reading and helping out in the tuckshop.' Ned's lips tilted in a smile, and Jemima couldn't help the laugh that began to bubble up from her chest.

'Tuckshop, really? I haven't heard that word for years.' She smiled as the memories came back. 'I remember my mum used to help out when I was at primary school. I loved the days she'd serve me and my friends.' Her smile disappeared as his words sunk in. 'But seriously? Surely there's some sort of confidentiality a bank manager should have?'

Ned shook his head. 'Not the bank manager's doing. Jenny Sykes, the bank teller, overheard the whole "Gwennie-Mummy" thing and got straight on the phone to the other Sykes women.' His expression got serious again. 'And it's worse than that. I've already had a call from my parents up on the north coast. Poor Mum was beside herself with happiness. Maisey Sykes is a friend of hers and couldn't wait to ring. Mum was cross at me, but she said she pretended to Maisey that she knew all the details. God knows what she told her.'

Jemima folded her hands in her lap. 'Well, we do have a situation, don't we?'

'We do. But I've given it a lot of thought. If we draw up a confidential agreement, one that just you and I know about—and we use an out-of-town solicitor—I think we can make this work. But only if you're absolutely comfortable with it, Jemmy.'

A number of emotions flitted through Jemima—not least the warmth that settled when he called her Jemmy—and she frowned. 'Tell me what you're thinking.'

'A marriage in name only, for one year. Of course, as far as we're concerned, but to the outside world, it would be real. I can't afford to jeopardise the loan. You'd move in, and that would free me up days and nights to get the farm working—that way, I might be able to get away with only hiring one farmhand—the kids would be happy, and with you being a "mum" and "wife" that will show those Sykes' women once and for all that you're here to stay.

'A year?'

Ned nodded slowly. 'I think a year will see me on my feet. The other thing is, if you're here all the time…well, I know what the town is like. You've already had experience with what they see as your glamorous reputation, and I think being married would fast track your acceptance back in the community, and you'd be able to get a teaching job when one comes up.'

'And then what?'

Ned frowned. 'That's the only thing that worries me. At the end of the year, we'd annul the marriage. It might hinder you from getting the job you want.'

Jemima waved a hand. 'We're in the twenty-first century. That can't be used as an excuse these days.'

'But this is Prickle Creek.'

'I'll worry about that when it happens.'

Ned's eyes widened. 'So you don't think it's a stupid idea?'

Jemima spoke slowly. 'I think we could make it work—the business side of things, I mean. The main thing that worries me is your kids. What would you tell them?'

'I know. Kids talk at school, and we don't want the real situation getting out. I'll have to think about that. Kelsey's already been upset about the idea of having a new mum.'

Jemima jerked her head up. 'You've already told them?'

'Of course not. It was when Gwennie said in the car that our new mum drove past us. Kelsey burred up, but we had a bit of a chat about you helping out. I've let the kids know that I already know you, so they don't wonder.'

'That sounds okay. Just play it as it comes. Be natural, and see how it works out.'

'So is that a yes?'

'I guess so.' Jemima smiled. Ned had visibly relaxed. 'The only thing I have to work out is what to tell my family.'

'We need to be truthful with those closest to us. When Mum and Dad come up, I'll tell them the truth, and I think you should do the same with Liam and Lucy.'

'We have a deal then.' Jemima held out her hand to seal the deal with a handshake. Ned took it and stared down at her bare fingers. As he held her hand, her chest filled with warmth, and her fingers tingled as he moved his head closer to hers. She tipped her head back a little and waited, wondering what he was thinking. God forbid, if he knew that she was hoping he'd seal the deal with a kiss. His lips opened, and his breath was warm on her cheek as he spoke.

'I'm sorry, Jemmy. I don't even have an engagement ring to offer you. We need to make this look real from the get-go.'

She waved her other hand and stood straighter, trying to dispel the stupid romantic notion that had flitted into her thoughts. She'd almost made a fool of herself. This was a business deal, and she had to remember that. 'Don't worry. I'm sure I have something at home.'

By the time Ryan woke up an hour later, Jemima and Ned had the details worked out. He'd called the courthouse in Dubbo and made an appointment for the following Friday. They had to attend the courthouse together and lodge a notice of intended marriage, and then they could be married a month later.

Jemima turned onto the gate of Prickle Creek Farm in a bit of a daze.

She was getting married.

Chapter Seven

One month later.

'Slowly, take it slowly. Use your knees.'

Kelsey grinned at Jemima as she rode Monty around the paddock next to the hay shed. The horse from Prickle Creek Farm was placid, and Jemima knew he would be fine for as long as Kelsey wanted to stay up there.

Liam had been more than happy to let her bring the old horse over, so both she and Kelsey had a mount to ride when Jemima moved in.

Tomorrow. Nerves skittered down her back as she watched Kelsey.

After she'd got home from Ned's place the afternoon he had talked about them getting married, she'd sat Liam and Angie down at Gran's kitchen table—funny how they all still referred to everything as Gran and Pop's even though they were touring the world—

and told them what was happening. The truth.

'That's old news; I already knew,' Angie said with a grin, but Liam's eyes widened.

'What?' he said. 'What do you mean you're getting married?'

Jemima nodded and gave Liam a sweet smile. 'Yep, I'm getting married, and don't go pulling the bossy big brother deal. I'm all grown up now.'

'Maisey Sykes asked me yesterday if you pair were getting married before Liam and I were.' Angie laughed and hugged Jemima. 'I managed to nod and smile and focus on her cat. The cat that had nothing wrong with it! She's such a gossip. I'm sure she came in just to get information out of me.' Angie had stepped back and kept hold of Jemima's hands. 'Don't worry, I played dumb.'

Liam and Angie, as well as Lucy and Garth, had gotten more used to the idea over the last month. Ned had hired Billy Andrews from Come-by-Chance to help him out, and he was working out well. Jemima had spent her days at the farm looking after Ryan, and she often stayed for dinner and helped the girls with their homework. To her relief, Ned had cooked each night. She hadn't had to admit her lack of cooking skills yet.

Liam had hitched up the horse float and helped her load Monty this morning. He stood beside the car window as she fastened her seatbelt. 'Are you sure about this, Jemmy?' Liam had followed her to the ute, and his brows had lowered as she started the engine. He hadn't been impressed when Jemima had filled him in on the details. 'I know Ned's a great bloke, but marrying him to help him out? And moving in with him and three kids? It's a bit over the top, isn't it? Are you really sure that you haven't rushed this? I know what a kind heart you have.'

'I'm a big girl now, Liam. You don't have to worry about me. Ned needed a big favour, and this was the best way to go about it for everyone. And I'm really grateful to you and Angie for looking after Ryan while we go to Dubbo tomorrow. And picking up the girls from school, too.'

'That's not a problem.' Liam had looked worried. 'I just don't want to see you get hurt.'

'No fear of that, big brother. My heart tells me I'm doing the right thing.'

Now, as she stood watching the look of delight on Kelsey's face, Jemima knew the first hurdle had been overcome. She'd made the right decision agreeing to Ned's 'proposal.' Both of them—business and marriage. When they'd sat down with his three children last night and told them that Jemima was coming to live with them on Saturday—they hadn't mentioned the *M* word yet—the only thing Kelsey had wanted to know was if she was bringing any more horses with her.

Gwennie had squealed and thrown herself into Jemima's lap and hugged her tightly. 'Oh, I am so happy,' she'd cried.

Ryan had looked at her for a minute and then smiled before he went back to playing with his cars. Jemima had watched as Ned let out the breath he'd been holding. She'd caught his eye, and when he'd smiled at her, a warm feeling had shimmied in her chest, and she'd looked away.

Oh no, you don't, she'd chastised herself silently. *Don't even think about going there.*

'Jemima!' Kelsey's call pulled her from her thoughts that were all over the place. 'Can I go faster? Can he canter?'

She walked over to the middle of the paddock, where Monty had stopped dead. Kelsey held onto the reins tightly as he put his head down and chewed on the only piece of green grass that was growing there.

'Monty's a bit old to go much faster. Maybe in a few weeks, we might go looking for a new horse. Maybe two? One for each of us. The farm could do with some more horses. What would you think about that?'

Kelsey's eyes lit up, and Jemima wondered if she was moving too quickly. She didn't want it to look like she was trying to buy Kelsey's affection. She probably should have asked Ned before she talked about buying a horse, but if he wasn't happy with the idea, she'd buy one and keep it over at Prickle Creek. She'd missed riding the years she'd been a model. And it would be fun to take Kelsey into pony club in Prickle Creek on Saturdays.

'I think that would be an amazing idea,' Kelsey said.

'Do you know how much time it takes to look after a horse? There's a lot of responsibility. You have to feed them and check they have water every day and keep their hooves trimmed.'

'Oh, I would love to do that. Do you think Daddy will let me?'

Maybe she should speak to Ned about it first. Jemima had noticed he was very protective of the children and even a bit overbearing about it. But living on a farm, they had to have freedom. She was looking forward to taking them yabbie fishing, swimming in the hot water bore, and simply letting them be kids in the fresh country air. She really needed to sit down and have a good talk with Ned. He'd grown up here. He would understand what she meant. She knew he'd been busy working since they'd arrived. He hadn't even finished unpacking. There were dozens of boxes lining the hallway to the bedrooms. She hadn't felt comfortable doing much in the house until she moved across. She'd mainly focused on helping the kids with their schoolwork, doing the dishes, and pegging the washing out. Gwennie had helped her out in the garden, and she'd promised to help her start a small herb and vegetable garden at the back of the house in a few weeks when the weather cooled down a bit. There was one thing that Jemima was sure about. There was so much to keep her busy; the next twelve months were going to fly by.

'Come on, we'd better hurry up. Liam and Angie have invited us all over to Prickle Creek Farm for dinner, and it's time you got ready. And I have to take the ute and horse float back.'

'Are there more horses over there? And other animals? Do

they have dogs?' Kelsey chattered away as Jemima took the saddle off Monty. 'Maybe they'd like one of our kittens? I so want to be a vet when I grow up.'

'Here, you take the blanket and put it in the shed while I take his bridle off.' Jemima smiled. She could almost see Kelsey's chest puff out with pride. It had only been a month since she'd met Ned's three beautiful children. The time she had spent with them had been amazing. For the first time since she'd left Prickle Creek to follow her career, she was appreciated for being herself. Someone needed her.

Just Jemima.

Ned was grateful she was helping him out, but she was getting as much out of the deal on her side. The kids were constantly asking her questions, and she was able to help them in so many ways, and she loved playing with them. Ryan loved hide and seek, and she pretended not to find him most of the time. He had the most gorgeous little giggle, and she knew where he was hiding because he could never keep quiet.

'There are a few more horses, but they're all work horses.' Jemima opened the gate and led Monty into the paddock, and then after she checked he had water, she slipped the chain over the hoop on the gate. Kelsey was swinging on the fence.

'Did you know that Angie is the vet in town?' Jemima asked.

'Really? That is so awesome.'

Jemima smiled. She was getting used to that word. It must be the current buzzword kids used when they liked something. She had so much to learn.

'Daddy will have to get a horse, too, for when he buys the cattle. If we all have one, I could help him in the paddocks. Grandpa only has one of those silly quad runners here.'

'I noticed that. I don't like them. They can be dangerous.' Jemima smiled as Kelsey slipped her hand into hers as they walked back to the house, and Jemima's heart swelled with affection for the almost-teenager. 'But you'll have to learn how to ride first.'

Progress was being made.

Ned showered while Ryan was in the bath and dressed in clean jeans and a white T-shirt that fitted snugly to his broad chest. He was combing Ryan's hair, and Jemima smiled to see that Ryan was dressed in jeans and a white T-shirt.

'You're optimistic.'

'Huh?' Ned's forehead wrinkled in a frown.

'The white T-shirt on Ryan.'

The crinkles beside Ned's eyes deepened. 'He chose it.'

'I'll head back over now. I'll see you all when you get over there.' Jemima picked up her bag and the ute keys. 'Liam asked me to take his ute back.'

'Thank you for bringing the horse over, Jemmy.' Ned

smiled, and Jemima noticed that the shadows beneath his eyes were not as dark as they'd been a few weeks ago.

'My pleasure. I'll see you all over at Prickle Creek in a while.'

'I feel bad not bringing anything with us. I've got a six-pack of beer in the fridge.'

'It's fine, but bring that if it makes you feel better. Gran's freezers are always stocked, and Lucy loves cooking. Did I you tell you Lucy and Garth are coming over, too?'

Ned nodded as Gwennie walked into the kitchen. 'Who's Lucy?'

'She's my cousin,' Jemima said with a smile.

'Will that make her my aunty when you and Daddy get married?'

Jemima raised her eyebrows and looked at Ned over Gwennie's head. She didn't think he'd told the children yet that they were getting married. Even though he hadn't said it in as many words, she knew he was worried about Kelsey's reaction.

He shook his head slightly and shrugged. 'Where did you hear that, Gwennie?'

'My teacher asked me when you were getting married, and I said Jemima was coming to live with us, so I guessed it was going to be soon.'

'Bloody Prickle Creek gossip mill,' Ned muttered beneath

his breath.

'Maybe before you come over, you should tell the children it's tomorrow?' she said quietly. They had decided to marry quietly at the courthouse in Dubbo, the closest town where they could have a civil ceremony. 'Best to be honest because, for all we know, we'll bump into someone from Prickle Creek in Dubbo!'

Gwennie switched the television on and was soon engrossed in cartoons. The noise covered their conversation as Ned took Jemima's elbow and walked her to the door. She ignored the funny shaky feeling that ran down her legs when his fingers brushed her skin.

'That's a good point. I'll sit them down when Kelsey gets out of the bathroom.' He held open the screen door as she walked onto the verandah. 'And thank you, Jemmy. I owe you so much.'

'Unless you promise to stop gushing gratitude every time we have a conversation, I might change my mind. It's not too late, you know.' She tempered her words with a smile. 'We're not married yet.'

'Okay, okay.' He put his hands up and laughed. 'One last time and then I'll stop. Thank you.'

'I'll see you at Prickle Creek.' Jemima stopped and turned as she reached the bottom step. 'Um, Ned. This might sound like a silly question, but what are you wearing tomorrow? I don't want to be over . . . or underdressed.'

Ned shrugged again. 'I hadn't thought about it yet. I guess whatever I can find clean in the wardrobe.'

Jemima walked to the car. 'As long as I know if it's jeans or a suit, I can choose what to wear.'

She regretted her words as soon as his smile faded.

Stupid. No need to remind him of his first wedding.

'Make it jeans. After all, this is the country,' she said gaily as she opened the car door.

***

Ned walked slowly back inside. Was he making a stupid mistake? Marrying Jemima tomorrow might solve his problems, but was he rushing into an easy solution for working the property? Maybe he should have toughed it out and tried to get a loan to hire some help through a broker in Sydney. When he'd come up with the idea, he hadn't given it enough thought. There were so many complications and others who were going to be affected by his actions. He should have thought of his children.

He walked through the living room and called down the hall, 'Come on, Kelsey. Hurry up.'

While he waited for his eldest daughter to appear, thoughts whirled around his head. This was his last chance to change his mind. Once he told them, there was no backing out. It was really out of character for him to be indecisive. Usually, once he settled on a course of action, he followed through. His whole life had been like that. The decision to leave the farm to go to university in Sydney, even though Dad would have loved for him to stay and take over, choosing his career path, marrying Cath, starting a family, and buying their home on the beach in Sydney. He'd always followed through once he'd made a decision—no second-guessing.

Hell, even the gut-wrenching and life-changing decision to turn off Cath's life support two months after the bloody car accident—when the doctors had told him there was no hope of recovery—he'd made that decision without the doubt that was plaguing him now. And like then, this decision would affect the well-being of his three children.

His fingers gripped the edge of the bench. It felt like a final step. Marrying Jemima—for whatever reason—was like closing the pages of his marriage to Cath. He'd vowed to himself the night of her funeral that he would never leave himself so vulnerable to grief again.

Ned clenched his jaw. Tomorrow wasn't a true marriage—even if they had to go through the vows—Jemima would be his wife in name only.

It was purely a business arrangement. An arrangement that meant he could spend more time with the kids and not need to juggle family and work. Whatever it took, he would do it. He and Jemima had travelled to Dubbo to see a solicitor before they went to the courthouse last month to file their intention of marriage. The solicitor had looked over the top of his glasses as he'd drawn up the agreement; they had both signed it, and now it was filed at the solicitor's office.

'I'm ready, Dad.' Kelsey walked into the kitchen.

'Gwennie, Ryan,' he called into the living room. 'Come into the kitchen. I want to talk to you before we go to Liam and Jemima's farm.'

Chapter Eight

Jemima had sat down with Lucy as she fed James in the nursery before the McCormacks arrived.

'Oh, my God, Jemmy. I'm so excited for you. I wish we could come to the wedding tomorrow.' Lucy smoothed her hand over baby James' soft cheeks as he nestled against her.

Jemima smiled. 'It's not a real wedding. We're getting married. But remember, the deal is top secret, okay? As far as Prickle Creek is concerned—and the kids—the marriage of Ned McCormack and Jemima Smythe is the real deal.'

Lucy grinned back at her as she stood. 'This young man has a wet nappy. You know you can trust me, Jemmy. I won't slip up. For the last month, I've dreamed it was the real thing for you.' She looked at Jemima from the corner of her eye as she put James on the change table. 'It wouldn't be such a bad thing, you know. Ned is quite a catch.'

'Don't even think about it.' Jemima stood. 'I'll go and get the food organised.' She knew that Lucy was looking at her curiously as she headed to the kitchen. The last thing she needed was for Lucy's romantic, happy-ever-after nature to kick in. She was having enough trouble ignoring the attraction that was building for Ned McCormack.

And his behaviour was confusing her, too.

Last week, Ryan insisted that Ned join in the game of hide and seek, which she was playing with the kids. She could smile now, but at the time, she hadn't known how to take it.

'One, two, eight, nine, ten, I'm coming, ready or not.' Ryan's little voice came from the kitchen as Jemima opened the door to the cupboard that housed the linen and the hot water system and slipped inside. She smiled as Gwennie immediately revealed her hiding spot behind the sofa by yelling out to Ryan that he couldn't count.

As the two children walked up the hall, Jemima stepped back and moved to pull the door further shut. She usually left it open a chink to give Ryan a clue. But when she stepped back, a chuckle warmed the back of her neck, and a pair of strong arms went around her.

'Looks like we chose the best hiding spot, Jemmy.'

Embarrassment—and something else pleasurable—surged through her as Ned held her close.

'Ssh, don't give us away,' he whispered as she tried to move away. 'He'll hear us.'

They stood close together as Ryan's little footsteps padded past the door. All sorts of thoughts skittered through Jemima's mind, and she held herself perfectly still and quiet. Ned had showered after he'd come in from the paddocks, and the fresh, masculine, clean smell surrounded her. She resisted temptation.

But it was so hard. All she wanted was to jump his bones.

Somehow, he must have picked up her thoughts. Mental telepathy in a cupboard? Those bones she was thinking about almost went to water as warm lips nuzzled the side of her neck.

'What are you doing?' she whispered as heat flooded through her.

There was laughter in his voice. 'It's easier to keep quiet if my lips are here.'

'Oh.'

Her head turned slowly and his warm lips slid along her cheek, getting closer to her mouth with every breath she took. Her legs trembled, and just as she reached to hold the hand that had snaked around her waist, he turned her in his arms.

His lips descended on hers, and when Jemima opened her mouth, Ned murmured against her lips. 'Excellent. Now we can both be perfectly quiet.'

His lips stayed on hers as little footsteps padded down the hall. Warm and soft, gentle, yet enticing.

The door flew open, and as light flooded into the cupboard, Jemima pulled away from Ned's hold. And those lips that set her legs trembling and the thoughts that ran rampant in her imagination.

'Found you!' Ryan giggled. 'You always hide in there, Jemmy!'

She fanned herself with her hand as she stepped into the hall. 'I'm pleased you found us; it was too hot in there.'

She could still hear Ned's amused chuckle as she'd taken Ryan's hand to help him find Kelsey. 'It sure was,' Ned had murmured.

Ever since then, she'd been so much more aware of him, but unsure how to take him.

'Jem?'

She jumped as Lucy's voice intruded on her thoughts as she came into the kitchen.

'Sorry, what did you say?'

'I said, I'm sure Maisey Sykes will come up with a story about you knowing each other in Sydney.'

'Um, yes. We'll leave it to Maisey.' Jemima smiled, her attention diverted as Ned drove in and parked near the shed. The three kids clambered out, and she could see the excitement on their faces as they ran across to the barbeque area. Ned walked more slowly behind them, his jeans moulding powerful thighs as he walked across the lawn. She forced herself to look away and pay attention to Lucy.

'Or Paris,' Jemima said as she turned away from the window.

'Paris?' Lucy screwed her nose up. 'Paris, what?'

'For the Sykes story,' Jemima said. 'But really, Ned and I met when we were kids when he used to play in Liam's treehouse. She wouldn't know that. She didn't live here then.'

'I must admit, when you told me, I wondered if you were making a huge mistake. If you were sure about what you were doing, but now that I've met Ned and the kids, I think it's fine. You're doing a good thing, you know, Jemmy. Missing out on that school job was meant to be.'

'It's all good. Anyway, it's only for a year, and it serves a purpose for both of us.' Jemima opened the fridge. 'What has to go outside?'

'The three bowls of salad.' Lucy took them from her as she passed them out. 'There's only one problem as far as I can see.'

'What's that?'

'Ned's a lovely guy, and the kids are sweet. How are you going to last a year without falling in love with the lot of them? That worries me, Jemmy. How will you feel about leaving them at the end of the year?'

Jemima laughed. 'There's no fear of that. It's a job, and that's what I'm treating it as. And besides, Ned's not my type.' She crossed her fingers behind her back.

Lucy frowned and didn't look convinced. 'What is your type?'

'I don't know. When I meet him, I'll tell you.' She opened the oven and took out the garlic bread. 'Come on, the meat'll be cooked by now. I'm starving.'

Liam, Garth, and Ned were out by the barbeque, and the two little girls walked over to the horse paddock, carrying Willow, Liam and Angie's pup. Jemima stood at the kitchen window, watching them as they balanced on the fence rail. She leaned forward and checked where Ryan was. She grinned when she spotted him playing in the red dirt at the back of the barbeque area. His once-white T-shirt was now streaked with red dirt.

As they walked out to the barbeque area to join the men and the children, Jemima smoothed her hair back.

'So, you're not nervous about making it real tomorrow? Or excited about being a bride?' Lucy asked quietly.

'No. I told you. It's just a job. I'm not a real bride; remember, it's a business arrangement.'

Lucy walked ahead and put the salads on the table. Jemima ignored the happiness that flooded through her when Ned looked up and smiled.

It's a job.

***

Catching up with Liam socially had been great, but Ned had sensed a little reticence when they'd first shaken hands. Even though he'd been at Daniela for more than a month, they'd both been too busy on their respective farms to catch up. They'd spoken a few times on the telephone but this was the first time they'd seen each other face-to-face. After dinner and a couple of beers, Liam had been up front about what was bugging him. Like he always had been. They'd walked over to the cattle crush and leaned against the rail, discussing the upcoming Prickle Creek cattle sale where Ned was going to buy his first stock. After a while, Liam put his beer on the top of the timber railing and looked at Ned.

'I'm not going to say much. I'm just going to ask one thing of you.'

Ned looked at him over his beer as he leaned on the fence. 'What's that?'

'Don't hurt my sister.'

'I won't. You have my word on that.'

'She comes across as tough, but she's not. She pretends she knows the world but she's done it tough.'

'What sort of tough?'

Liam shook his head. 'I'll let Jemmy tell you. If she wants to share.'

Ned didn't reply. He leaned back against the rail and looked over at the house. Ryan was still playing in the dirt—that boy would have the best resistance to germs—and would need another bath before bed. Just as well they had the underground bore at the farm to keep the water supply up. Gwennie was sitting at the table talking to Liam's fiancée, Angie, and Kelsey was being Jemmy's shadow as she had been ever since she'd discovered Jemima was as mad keen on horses as she was.

The problem would be what he could do for her.

Liam looked at him curiously as they walked back to the barbeque area. 'You're quiet, mate.'

'Just thinking. Will you be at the cattle sales next Thursday?' Ned pulled his thoughts back to the present. 'I'd appreciate an experienced cattle buyer with me.'

Liam laughed. 'Well, I'm not that experienced. I've only been back here a few months myself. But I'm happy to come and help you as best I can. Shame our Pop's not home yet. He's the one with the cattle experience. I'm still learning.'

'When I was here as a kid, I never took much notice of what Dad was doing.' He shook his head with a rueful laugh. 'Never planned to be back out here on the land.'

'Me neither. Are you here to stay?' Liam asked as they walked across to the house. The sun was setting and the sky was a glorious mix of pinks and gold. But Ned didn't take much notice of it. All he thought of was the number of chores he had waiting for him at home.

He shrugged. 'At the moment, that's the plan. As long as I can make the farm a going concern.'

Jemmy was clearing the table and a puff of wind lifted her

loose hair in a blonde tangle around her head. The setting sun was behind her and she was silhouetted in a halo of soft light; not that she needed anything to make her look more attractive. Every time Ned looked at her, he couldn't believe what a beautiful woman she was. Her knee-length dress was printed with brightly coloured flowers and as he watched, she put her head back and laughed at something Kelsey said to her. She was vital and alive and beautiful, and something shifted in him.

Full of life.

Anticipation grew for the next year; a certainty that Jemima's presence would make a difference to the children. She gave him renewed hope that life could be happy, and more than anything, her being there would provide the opportunity for him to get out on the farm and make a go of it. A chance to provide a good and happy life for his children. The next year would set the foundation for the future. He smiled; it was going to be a great year. The thought of having Jemmy in the house with them for a year stirred feelings that he knew he'd have to keep a lid on. It was only because she was such a beautiful woman.

That's all it is. Any red-blooded male would be feeling the same attraction that he was. He would have to be careful, that's all. The last thing he wanted to do was frighten her off.

Even though Jemima said she didn't want anything, Ned vowed that when the year was up, he would find something that she wanted, and he'd show his gratitude for what she was doing for his family.

'Ned. A coffee?' Angie caught his attention as she carried out a tray with a cake on it. He dragged his gaze away from Jemima.

'Thanks, but no. I'll get these kids home.' He glanced across at Jemima. 'We've got an early start tomorrow.'

'Daddy, can we *pwease* have some cake before we go?' Ryan tugged on his shirt.

Ned looked down, groaned, and held his hand out. 'You can as long as you wash those hands first. Come on.'

'I'll take him, Daddy. If I wash my hands can I have some cake, too?' Gwennie asked.

'Of course, sweetie. Kelsey, I suppose you want cake?'

'Of course I do, and I was going to ask Jemima if she'd teach me how to make it.'

Liam and Lucy burst out laughing and Ned looked at them curiously. 'What's so funny?'

Jemima folded her arms and glared at them but her glare was softened when her lips lifted in a half-smile.

'Oh, dear,' Liam spluttered. 'Ned, maybe you didn't do your homework well enough.'

'Homework? What homework?'

Lucy nudged Jemima. 'It's a well-known fact in our family

that Jemmy can't even boil water. She obviously hasn't done any cooking at your place yet.'

'No, she hasn't,' Ned said slowly. 'I didn't think it was fair when she had the house to organise, and the laundry, and look after Ryan until I came in.'

Liam slapped his thigh. 'And I'll bet you didn't insist, did you, Jemmy?'

Ned's lips twitched as Jemima drew herself to her full height and glared at her brother.

'You have no idea what I've learned over the past five years, Liam Smythe. For all you know I could be a gourmet chef now.'

Liam chuckled and batted away Jemima's finger as she poked it into his chest.

'So can you cook, now, can you, sis?'

'Sort of,' she said with the glimmer of a smile.

Lucy turned to Kelsey. 'You can come over to our place, Kelsey, and I'll teach you how to bake cakes, if you like.'

'I might come, too,' Jemima said before she turned to Ned. 'Don't worry. I can do the basics. No one will starve.'

'Any cooking is an improvement on mine,' he said with a laugh. 'The kids will vouch for that.'

Lucy grinned. 'Liam could teach you, too. Did you know he won the blue ribbon for the "cake of the show" at the last Prickle

Creek show?'

Jemima's peal of laughter made Ned smile. 'Oh, is that for real, Liam? I wish I'd known that.'

'It was only because Lucy was in hospital having James. It won't happen again,' Liam said. 'Gran's record was at stake. You can do it this year, Jemmy, if Gran and Pop are still tripping around.'

Ned leaned over and nudged Liam. 'I'm impressed, mate. "Cake of the show," hey? The only cake my poor kids ever get these days is from the bakery. So, I might come to Lucy's kitchen and learn, too.'

Gwennie frowned and looked up at him. 'But you won't need to, Daddy. When you and Jemima get married tomorrow, she'll be there to make the cakes and cook our tea.'

Jemmy grinned at him and leaned down to hug Gwennie. 'And I'll be there to teach little girls . . . *and* boys . . . that a woman can do anything a man can do and vice versa.'

After the cake was eaten, Ned gathered up his three children. 'Time to go home, kids.'

He thanked Liam and Angie for the invitation over and said goodbye to Garth and Lucy, who insisted that the next get-together would be at their farm.

Jemima walked over to the car with him and opened the door while he lifted a sleepy Ryan into the car seat in the back.

After Gwennie planted a smacking kiss on Jemima's cheek, Kelsey asked shyly whether Jemmy would mind if she kissed her goodnight, too. He smiled.

'Of course, you can.' He waited as Jemima hugged Kelsey, and his eldest followed her sister into the car.

Ned turned to Jemima, feeling awkward for the first time. 'I'll bring Ryan over as soon as the girls catch the bus in the morning. About eight-thirty?'

'That sounds like a plan. It's a good two hours to Dubbo and the appointment is for noon. Better allow for road works.'

'Yep, noon it is.' It seemed strange to be discussing a marriage as prosaically as though it was the weather. They stood there awkwardly for a while and then Ned opened the car door. 'See you tomorrow, then.'

'Yes. Tomorrow. Bye.' Jemima leaned down and waved to the kids through the window. Ryan was already asleep. 'See you tomorrow afternoon, girls.'

Jemima stood and watched the car until the taillights disappeared around the curve just before the cattle grid.

Tomorrow. Tomorrow she was marrying Ned McCormack and becoming a part of his life and the lives of his children.

What was marriage to Ned going to be like?

Am I making a mistake? Is it a knee-jerk reaction to not getting the job at the school?

Apart from helping both of them achieve the outcomes that they each needed, they were going to be living together twenty-four-seven.

Jemima shook her head and turned back to the house with a smile.

It was going to be fine. There was nothing to be gained from worrying about the unknown.

Chapter Nine

The following morning dawned bright and clear. Jemima stood in front of the small wardrobe in the spare bedroom at Gran and Pop's, trying to decide what to wear. All of her really good clothes were still in her unit at Mosman on the harbour in Sydney. She'd thought about selling the unit, but until she knew what the next year was going to bring, it was a bit of security for her. And she didn't need the money from either a sale or rental income. If no local teaching jobs came up, maybe she'd have to go back to Sydney to pursue the career she had her heart set on. And it was there if she ever needed to visit Sydney—or get away.

She stood there for a few minutes before her gaze settled on the outfit at the far end of the wardrobe. Not too dressy, but suitable for an occasion such as today's—she swallowed as she thought of what was ahead—her wedding.

Perfect.

Jemima nodded and laid the clothes out on the bed while she headed for the shower. Years of quick changes and being made up had made her a whiz at getting ready quickly, and it was only ten minutes later that she was putting the last touch of mascara on her eyes when she heard the rattle of a diesel engine pull up outside. With a deep breath, she smoothed down her silk top and walked into the living room.

Angie's eyes widened, and Liam whistled. 'Very nice, sis.'

Jemima frowned. 'I'm not too dressed up, am I?'

'No. You look lovely. I've hardly seen you in anything but jeans and T-shirts since I met you.' Angie held her arms out for a hug. 'It's perfect for a business meeting or a wedding.'

Ned lifted Ryan from the ute and carried him up the steps. Ned was quiet, and his only greeting to Angie was a brief nod and a quick good morning. He handed over the bag of spare clothes and toys to Ryan.

Ryan seemed happy enough to stay with Liam and Angie. Angie had taken the day off from her surgery to help out. As Ned held the door of the ute open for Jemima, the little boy waved goodbye. Jemima swallowed and put her hands on her lap as they backed out of the driveway. For the first time in a long time, she was tempted to chew her fingernails.

The trip to Dubbo was silent at times, apart from comments about the weather or the occasional remark about a particularly lush paddock of pasture. Jemima was lost in her thoughts, and Ned seemed just as preoccupied.

She jumped when he spoke as they slowed down for road works.

'When did you want to bring your gear over?'

'My gear?'

'Your clothes and stuff.'

'Oh. Tonight, I suppose.'

Silence again, and then they both spoke at the same time.

'What—' she said.

'Where—' he said.

Jemima glanced over at him. 'Are we going to spend a year doing this?'

'Doing what?' Her heart kicked up a beat as he took his eyes from the road briefly and smiled. Ned's simple smile made it so much easier for her to talk to him. Most of the time, she didn't know what was going on in his head. He always looked so damned serious.

'Being awkward with each other. Hedging around each other, being polite. It's going to be a very slow year if I have to think about what I say before I speak every time.'

'I know what you mean.'

She glanced down at his hand as he felt for the water bottle he'd put on the seat. Before he found it, Jemima picked it up, popped the cap, and passed it over.

'Thank you.' He tipped it up, and she watched as he drank, keeping his eyes on the road. He passed the bottle back over, and she put it in the console between the seats.

'So, what do you think? I guess it's a pretty unusual

arrangement we've made, and we don't want it to be any harder than it has to be.'

'Let's go back a few years and work from there. After all, you've been friends with Liam since you started primary school, so you probably met me when I was toddling around.' Jemima folded her arms.

Ned stared ahead at the straight road that stretched ahead of them. 'The only thing I remember was how you used to sit at the bottom of the tree in your backyard where Liam had his tree house.' Ned laughed. 'He used to pull the ladder up so you couldn't climb up. But you were persistent. You'd sit there for ages. Most of the time, you were still there when we came back down.'

'I loved his tree house. That big old tree blew over in a storm just before I started high school.'

'I didn't know that.' Ned shook his head. 'Once I started high school, I didn't come back into town much. Dad needed me around the farm. If I wasn't out helping him, I had my nose in the books because I was determined I wasn't going to be a cattle and wheat farmer.' He gave a rueful smile. 'And look at me now. Back on the land, trying to make it work. Last thing I ever expected I'd be doing.'

Jemima was torn. Ned seemed happy to talk, but she didn't want to introduce a topic that would make him sad. 'What sort of job did you do in the city?' she finally asked.

He must have sensed her reticence. 'It's okay. If we're going to be natural around the kids, you need to know these things. I was a construction manager for an international firm. We specialised in refurbishing shopping centres in cities.'

'So, you travelled a bit?'

'Yes, that went with the job. When the girls were little, I was away a lot.' Jemima noticed his hands tightening on the steering wheel, but he kept talking. 'I didn't realise how much I'd missed out on until'—he paused and took a breath— 'until I was a sole parent. Ryan was only three months old then.'

'I hated the travel in my job.' Jemima deliberately changed the subject. 'Everyone thought it was such a glamorous career. But being in a hotel room, living out of a suitcase, then sitting for hours while makeup was painted on your face, and then dealing with it being scrubbed off because the look wasn't right for the clothes.'

Ned laughed. 'It sounds as exciting as deciding whether a shoe shop should go next to a bookstore or a phone store. I learned a lot about marketing in those days. And you know what, now that the loan's through and Billy's started work, I'm beginning to think that being a farmer's not so bad.'

'I know what you're saying.' Jemima half-turned in the seat and tucked her legs beneath her. 'I was so excited when Gran called us back to Prickle Creek last year. Not that I told anyone that. They all thought I'd turned into a prima donna model. I wanted to see if home was as good as I remembered before I committed myself to staying here. Or whether it was just childhood memories.'

'And was it? Good, I mean?'

'Oh, yes.' Jemima frowned as Ned slowed the four-wheel drive. She looked ahead. They were entering the fifty-kilometre zone at the edge of town. They drove past a few housing estates and through two sets of traffic lights; she smiled as Ned took a close look at the shopping plaza close to the centre of town as they drove past.

He caught her looking and shrugged. 'I can't help myself. It's funny, you know, it's almost like living in a parallel dimension. When I'm in the city, I almost forget I'm a farmer.'

'I know exactly what you mean. When I went back to Sydney for a week after Christmas, it was like being in an alien environment.' She looked across at Ned. 'If you ever want to take the kids back to Sydney for a visit, I've got a perfectly good apartment sitting empty on the harbour.'

'Thank you. I might take you up on that. They still have one set of grandparents in the city, and we should visit when I get on top of things out here.' Ned slowed the ute down. 'Here we are. I'll park at the back of the courthouse. I noticed a car park the last time we were here.'

Jemima sat up straight in the seat and surreptitiously wiped her hands on the side of her trousers. Ned had dressed casually, too, but he wore a plain-coloured shirt, rather than a checked one, for a change, and the shirt was tucked into his jeans. He wore a smart leather belt, and his riding boots had been polished to a high shine. Not too casual, but not overdressed.

Even though it was a business arrangement, it was still a wedding. It was nice to see that Ned had made an effort to look nice. Jemima had chosen a simple pair of linen trousers and a sleeveless silk shirt in a pale green.

He pulled the ute into a parking space near the entrance, and Jemima took a deep breath as he walked around and opened the door.

'Ready?' He held out his hand, and she took it as she stepped out of the car.

As ready as I'll ever be.

***

Both Jemima and Ned had forgotten that they needed two witnesses for the ceremony. While the celebrant waited, they looked at each other, eyes wide.

Jemima put her hand to her mouth as embarrassment flooded her. 'Oh, we're so sorry. My family are minding the children'—heat rushed to her face as the woman smiled— 'and we never gave it another thought after you mentioned it the other day.'

Ned hurried across to the door. 'Give me five minutes. I'll be back.'

Jemima watched curiously as he slipped through the door and closed it behind him. *Where was he going?*

The celebrant stood. 'Ring the buzzer when you're ready, and I'll come back out.' She glanced at her watch. 'I don't have another ceremony for forty-five minutes, so we have plenty of time.'

Jemima wondered how many people came into this impersonal government building to get married and what their reasons were. Was the business arrangement that she and Ned made a common occurrence? Why else would you get married here?

As a teenager, she'd dreamed of her wedding day, a white frothy wedding dress, a diamond tiara, and all her family around her. Strangely, the groom had never really entered her dreams. The closest she'd ever got to a wedding dress was the dozens of designer wedding dresses she'd modelled over the past five years. With a sad sigh, she looked around. The smell of mouldy carpet and the bright light from fluorescent lighting provided a very different setting to the one she'd dreamed of. Nerves tugged at her, and she swallowed, more nervous than she'd ever been when she'd modelled in front of hundreds of people.

Jemima jumped as the door creaked open, and a tiny old

woman in a floral dress and a straw hat with flowers around the crown stepped into the waiting room, closely followed by Ned and an elderly gentleman in an old-fashioned suit.

The woman held a small posy of flowers in one hand, and she held out her free hand to Jemima as she hurried across the faded carpet.

'Oh, my dear. Look how much you've grown! And how beautiful you are!' She turned to the man in the suit. 'Isn't she, Alfred?'

Jemima stood and accepted the hand that was held out to her. She towered over the little lady. She looked to Ned with her eyebrows raised.

Who are these people?

'Jemmy, you remember Mrs McGillicuddy?' Ned smiled, and Jemima's mouth dropped open as she looked down at the elderly lady who was smiling up at her.

'Mrs. McGillicuddy? I haven't seen you since you taught me in kindergarten!'

'Please call me Ethel.' Her voice was high-pitched as it always had been in the classroom, and Jemima shook her head as she looked back at Ned.

'I don't think I've seen either of you since you were little children.' The elderly woman's eyes sparkled as she looked around. 'And now I get to come to your wedding.'

'I noticed Mr and Mrs M in the foyer when we came into the building,' Ned explained. 'And I thought it would be nice to have someone we both knew to witness our wedding. Luckily, they had the time to help us out.'

'Your grandmother told me you were coming home to Prickle Creek the last time I saw her at the CWA meeting,' Mrs McGillicuddy tutted. 'But she didn't tell me you were engaged to Ned McCormack. Wait till I talk to her!'

Uh oh. Another quick phone call she'd have to make before the day was up. Gran and Pop wouldn't be happy if they heard about the wedding on the local grapevine. All Jemima could hope was that they were still out of phone service. Last time she'd tried to call to tell them they'd been incommunicado.

The door to the office opened, and the celebrant came back into the room.

'Good. All ready, then?'

Jemima's mouth dried. All of a sudden, with the McGillicuddys in their old-fashioned clothes and Ethel pressing the flower posy into her hand, she felt as though she'd fallen down a rabbit hole.

'I've finished with the flowers, so you can have them now.'

'Finished with them?' Jemima asked, and damn if her voice didn't come out in a high-pitched squeak, too.

'Yes.' Ethel looked up at her husband and winked. 'Alfred

and I decided to renew our vows. It's our sixtieth wedding anniversary today. And isn't it wonderful that you and Ned will share it with us?'

As Ned squeezed her hand gently, Jemima felt like an absolute fraud. Her breath hitched as she wondered why on earth she had agreed to do this. Ned leaned over, and his warm breath brushed her ear as he whispered.

'Take a deep breath, Jemmy. It's okay.'

Jemima took a deep breath as he directed and clutched the flower posy in her left hand. Ned led her to the small area at the side of the office where two pairs of plastic chairs had been arranged near a small stand.

Think of the children. Think of how I'm helping Ned out. Think of—

'Thank you. Let's get started.' The celebrant's voice interrupted her thoughts.

Ethel and Alfred sat in the chairs to the left of them, and Ned and Jemima stood in front of the celebrant. Ned held her hand tightly, and she wondered for a moment if he was worried she was going to make a run for it.

What was the name of that movie she and Lucy had loved to watch in their teens? The one where the bride took off at each wedding? Jemima bit back a smile as she imagined pulling free from Ned's hand, clambering over the plastic chairs, pushing open the door and running down the corridor. Nowhere near as romantic as the fleeing bride on horseback.

The celebrant smiled and began to speak. 'My name is Barbara Deevers, and I am duly authorised by law to solemnise marriages according to law. Before you are joined in marriage in my presence and in the presence of these two witnesses,'—she nodded to Ethel and Alfred with a smile—'I am to remind you of the solemn and binding nature of the relationship into which you are now about to enter. Marriage, according to law in Australia, is the union of a man and a woman to the exclusion of all others, voluntarily entered into for life.'

Jemima's heart sank. *For life. Oh, dear.*

Ned leaned over, and his breath whispered on her cheek this time. 'It's okay.'

The next five minutes were a blur for Jemima as she and Ned agreed to be the lawfully wedded husband and wife of each other, the requisite paperwork was signed, and the marriage certificate was handed to Ned.

Jemima jumped as Ethel's squeaky voice demanded that the groom must now kiss the bride. Before she could think, Ned's arms went around her, and cool, firm lips pressed briefly against hers. A ripple of heat warmed her skin, and Ned's hand pressed into the small of her back. She looked up into a pair of dancing brown eyes, and the warmth in Ned's expression calmed her.

'Well, we've done it, Jemmy. We're married.' He lowered his head, and this time, she saw the kiss coming. She opened her lips slightly as he pressed his mouth against hers.

'Thank—'

Jemima shook her head, and the sensation of Ned's lips sliding gently against hers set butterflies fluttering in her tummy. She pressed her hand against his chest and pulled her head back a little bit. 'No more thanking me. You promised, remember?'

'I do.' He smiled, and the butterflies in her tummy fluttered harder. His lips felt as good as she'd remembered from when they'd hidden in the linen cupboard a couple of weeks back. The hard part was going to be forgetting.

'Are you having a wedding lunch?' Ethel asked as she smiled at them.

'Um . . .' Jemima looked at Ned.

He nodded. 'I think that's an excellent idea. Alfred and Ethel, would you like to make it a double'—he glanced at Jemima with his eyebrows raised— 'celebration?'

Chapter Ten

Ned knew that Jemima had been on edge in the courthouse, but the arrival of the McGillicuddys had seemed to settle her nerves. Lunch at the old hotel on the corner of the main street had been fun, and after a while, she'd relaxed and they'd shared school memories and laughs with the elderly couple.

Ethel seemed to know his background, but she didn't delve too much, and he was grateful when she asked how old his children were.

Prickle Creek was a small town, and there wasn't a lot that was private. He'd received many sympathy cards from the locals after the funeral.

Jemima didn't fare so well, but she handled herself well when Ethel asked her how she felt about taking on a ready-made family.

'Oh, I'm sure I'll be fine. The children are wonderful, and I love spending time with them.' She caught Ned's eye, and a strange feeling settled in his stomach. The jolt of desire that had shafted through him when he'd kissed her in the registry office had been a shock. Her lips had been soft beneath his. He'd had to try really hard to resist kissing her ever since they'd played hide and seek with Ryan the other night. Jemima's eyes were shining, and he realised that she meant every word she was saying. 'I think it's going to be better than being a teacher. After having the kiddies in your class for a whole year, it must be so hard to hand them over to the next teacher at the end of the year.'

Ned smiled as Jemima neatly turned the conversation over to the retired teacher, and they talked about teaching for the rest of lunch.

'Some kiddies you love to hand over at the end of the year.' Ethel shook her head as she laughed, and her cheeks wrinkled even more. 'Your cousin, Sebastian, was one of them. I thought that boy would be the death of me. The practical jokes he used to play. Even in kindergarten!'

As they left the hotel an hour later, Ned shook Alfred's hand, and Ethel leaned over and whispered in Jemima's ear. As his new wife dropped her head, her cheeks flamed bright red, but her lips were lifted in a smile.

'We'd better get a move on, so we're home before dark.' Ned kissed Ethel's cheeks and took the arm of a still-blushing Jemima.

Ned frowned, worried that their business arrangement had been revealed somehow. If Paul Crowe had gotten wind of the fact that their marriage was not the real deal, the loan would have been in jeopardy. Prickle Creek was too small to let the truth out to anyone.

The sky had clouded over while they were inside and a hot wind was blowing from the west. He kept his hand on Jemima's elbow until they were around the corner and out of the McGillicuddys' sight.

'Was everything okay back there?' he asked.

Jemima glanced up at him with a nervous smile. 'Back where?'

'In the hotel when Ethel whispered to you.'

Her cheeks coloured again.

'Oh no.' Ned put one hand up to his eyes. 'Don't tell me the game's up already?'

To his surprise, the sound that came from Jemima's lips was a cross between a giggle and a snicker. More like something he was used to from his girls.

'Well?' He stopped walking as they reached the entrance to the car park. 'What is it? What are you smiling at? What's so funny?'

He tipped his head to the side and stared at her. 'Please tell me I don't have anything to worry about.'

'You don't. They think we're a couple. I can guarantee that.' Her cheeks were still flushed, but her eyes were dancing. 'I'm merely embarrassed because of what my kindergarten teacher said to me.'

Ned frowned. 'What did Ethel say? You went bright red.'

This time, Jemima did giggle, and Ned couldn't help smiling. 'Come on, Jemmy. Spill.'

'She took my hand in hers and told me she had something very important to tell me. She said it was the secret of their sixty years of happy marriage.'

'Do I really want to know this?' Ned took her hand. 'Come on. I'm not going to let go until you share with me.'

Jemima leaned forward, and a whiff of her perfume tickled his nose. 'She told me to make sure that I looked after you.'

'That's sweet of her.'

'*Really* looked after you.' Another giggle bubbled out. 'Then she told me that a man has needs, and if I made sure I looked after *all* your needs, she could guarantee us sixty years together, too.'

'Oh my God. I hope I don't run into them in town. I'll never look at Ethel McGillicuddy the same way again.'

'I almost said we were business only and then I realised I couldn't. And then she asked me if I was pregnant and if that was why we were getting married before Gran and Pop came home!'

'Oh, the joys of living in a small town.' Ned shook his head, but he was enjoying this light side of Jemima. 'We will have to be careful, especially around the kids. You know what Gwennie's like.' Ned kept hold of her hand as they walked to the car. 'We'd better sort some things out in the car on the way home.' He opened the door and waited for her to climb in. 'There you go, Mrs McCormack.'

***

Mrs McCormack.

A strange feeling settled in Jemima's chest, and she clasped her hands together in her lap. Suddenly, what they had planned and discussed for the past month was real. Every time when they had talked about their 'business arrangement,' Ned had been polite…no, that wasn't the right word.

Jemima frowned.

He'd been pleasant but distant.

But today, Ned had been different. The barrier that was usually there was gone. He'd been warm and friendly. And he'd smiled a lot more.

Much more relaxed.

Much easier to talk to.

This was a different Ned she was going to have to get used to. Especially since tonight, when they got back to Prickle Creek, she'd be taking most of her things across to Ned's farm. It had to look real; it had to look as though she was going there for good. It was no use just packing a suitcase as though she was only going for a visit.

Gwennie didn't miss a trick, and the last thing they wanted

was for her to blab at school that Jemima wasn't really married to her dad.

Jemima stared through the car window as they turned onto the highway and headed back towards home. The afternoon was fading, and the lowering sun was bathing the ghost gum trees in a soft orange light. The usually white trunks were a soft apricot. Smoke haze lingered in the treetops from a fire west of town, and the clouds were tinged with golden hues.

'It's going to be a pretty sunset.' Ned's words echoed her thoughts.

'We should be home before dark.' Jemima turned to look at him. One hand was on the steering wheel and the other was tapping on his thigh in time with the music playing softly on the radio.

'You look…relaxed.'

Ned turned with a smile. 'I am. It was good to get that out of the way. And having lunch with the McGillicuddys was fun.'

Jemima swallowed.

Out of the way.

Just as well she had no emotional investment in this marriage or that comment would have stung. She sat up straight in the seat, ignoring the little kernel of hurt that lodged in her stomach.

'Yes.' Her voice was firm. 'That's out of the way. Now,

only twelve months to go, and it will be done and dusted.'

Ned's glance was curious. 'You sound like you can't wait for the time to go.'

Jemima waved a casual hand to cover up the funny ache in her chest. 'No, not at all. It's going to be fun looking after the children.'

And it would be. Jemima couldn't think of anything she'd rather be doing for the next year.

Apart from getting a full-time teaching job.

***

Prickle Creek Farm was lit up like a Christmas tree when Ned pulled the ute up near the house gate just after sunset. When he turned off the engine, voices and laughter drifted out of the house on the still evening air. He opened the door and went around to open Jemima's door.

As he waited, she reached down for the posy of flowers that she had held during the ceremony. She leaned forward, and a loose strand of hair slipped from the clip. Before he could think, he reached over and tucked it behind her ear. Jemima stilled as she moved back with the flowers, and his hand froze.

'Sorry, habit with the kids.'

'I'll put these flowers in a jar of water. They're so pretty it would be a shame to see them wither.'

'Jemmy?' Ned kept his voice soft.

She swung her legs out of the car and looked up at him as he held his hand out. 'Yes?'

'Look, I know it wasn't a real wedding, but I want to tell you how lovely you looked today.' He rushed on, feeling like a bit of an idiot as a slight pink rose in her cheeks. God, how many people would tell her in a working day how beautiful she was?

She was a model, for goodness' sake, you jerk.

But Jemima squeezed his hand as she took it, and he helped her down from the high seat of the ute. 'Thank you. Even though it wasn't a real wedding, I did have fun.'

'That's a good start for the rest of the year, then,' he said. She held his gaze and nodded.

'Daddy, Daddy.' The front screen door burst open, and Ryan ran out, closely followed by the two girls, and the moment was gone.

Just as well, Ned thought. It wasn't the right thing to do, getting all soppy about a business arrangement. He dropped Jemmy's hand and closed the door behind her as they walked over to the steps together.

'Looks like you're all ready to go home. Have you been good for Liam and Angie?' Ned asked as Ryan tried to climb up his legs. He bent down and swung his little boy up into his arms. His hair was wet, and his face was scrubbed clean. '*Mmm*, you smell like . . . apples?'

Kelsey folded her arms as she waited on the top of the steps. Angie took us to feed the pigs, and Ryan fell in the mud.'

Jemima caught Ned's eye and they shared a smile. 'That doesn't sound like Ryan.'

'Oh, yes, it does, Jemmy,' Gwennie piped up. 'He's always getting in the dirt.'

'I've noticed,' Jemima replied as she reached out for Gwennie's hand. Ned watched as his little girl took it without hesitation. Over the past month, both of the girls had accepted Jemima.

'Come on, you pair.' Kelsey tapped her foot at the top of the stairs. 'We have a surprise.'

'We have *bwekfast,*' Ryan squealed and bounced up and down in Ned's arms.

'Ryan! Don't spoil it!' Gwennie said.

'Breakfast?' Ned asked. 'It's teatime.'

The door opened again. 'Come inside, everyone.' Angie held the door open as Gwennie and Kelsey hurried inside.

She glanced at Ned, and her smile was half apologetic. 'I'm sorry; I know you're probably in a hurry to get back home, but the girls really wanted to do this.' Angie held her arms out to Ryan, and he almost jumped out of Ned's hold. 'We'll go first and'—she glanced at Jemima— 'you pair, wait a minute and then come in when we call you.'

She disappeared inside with Ryan on her hip, and he glanced over at Jemima with his eyebrows raised.

'What do you suppose they're up to?' she asked.

Ned chuckled. 'Honestly? With those girls, you never know.'

As they waited, the soft strains of orchestral music drifted out through the door, followed by Kelsey calling, 'You can come in now.'

Ned shrugged. He held open the door for Jemima and followed but bumped into her as she stopped dead in the doorway to the kitchen. *'Here Comes the Bride'* played from a phone propped up on the table.

His three children, Liam and Angie, were sitting at the table.

A table that had been decorated with more flowers than he'd seen for a long time and in the middle sat a huge cake. Ned swallowed as he looked at his children. Their faces were beaming, and his chest tightened. They looked *happy*.

All the doubts he'd had about this business arrangement fled, and he reached down for Jemima's hand. He felt her tense as he took it.

'This is *bwekfast*, Daddy. At night. And we get cake, too!' Ryan's voice was the usual high-pitched squeal.

'A wedding breakfast,' Gwennie added.

'Come and sit down,' Angie said. 'We have champagne and cake.'

***

Ned led Jemima across to the table, and he kept hold of her hand as they stood there, looking at the yellow and red roses that were scattered on the white damask cloth. Little frissons of nerves kept tingling up her arm and down into her chest as he smiled at his children.

'We made a wedding breakfast for you and Jemmy, Daddy,' Gwennie said.

'And *we* cooked the cake,' Kelsey said. 'Liam helped us follow the recipe while Angie showed Ryan the pigs. Liam won a ribbon for cooking cakes at the show, you know.'

'I heard that Liam knows how to cook cakes.' Jemima shot a grateful grin at her brother, pleased that Liam and Angie were supporting them in making this marriage the real thing in front of the kids.

'Never thought I'd help make a wedding cake for my little sister, though.' Liam winked at the girls and they both giggled.

Ned held the chair out for her, and she sat down. Liam popped the cork from a champagne bottle. Angie opened a bottle of lemonade for the children and cut the cake into slices.

Once he'd filled the glasses, Liam held up his. 'To Ned and Jemmy. May . . . may your marriage be all that you want.'

Jemima jumped as Ned reached for her hand beneath the table and squeezed it.

'Thank you, all,' he said. 'Thank you for a lovely celebration. It's been a good day, hasn't it, Jemmy?'

Jemmy bit her lip, unable to believe that she felt like crying. A warm, happy feeling filled her chest, and for a minute, she could almost believe this was real. 'It's been a lovely day.' She picked up her glass and frowned as the bubbles tickled her nose. The last time she'd had champagne was in New York. It seemed like a million miles away from this farmhouse.

'Hurry up and eat your cake, kids.' Ned let go of her hand. 'It's time we went home.'

Home. Jemima took a deep breath. Home for them and a temporary workplace for her.

All they had to do was keep the charade up until Ned was back on his feet and the farm was in the black again.

She stood and pushed her chair back. 'I'll go and get my things.'

The big smiles on the girls' faces pushed her doubts away a little as she headed for her room.

Chapter Eleven

Even though it was only a five-minute drive, Ryan nodded off to sleep in the ute on the way across to the farm.

'Scooter off and have your showers while I put Ryan to bed,' Ned instructed the girls when he lifted Ryan out of the car seat. He strode up the steps with the girls following close behind. Jemima went around to the back of the ute and pulled out her two suitcases. Angie had almost stopped her putting them in the back of the tray with the chaff bags, dog food, and hay bales.

'Jemmy, they're Louis Vuitton, for goodness' sake. You can't put them in a farm ute.'

Jemima kept her voice matter-of-fact. She'd seen the strange look on Ned's face when he'd glanced at the labels on the monogrammed canvas bags with the glossy brass corners and clips.

'They're just suitcases, Angie.' But the fact that each suitcase had cost a few thousand dollars, and she hadn't given it a thought at the time, brought home the different lifestyle that Ned had been living for the past few months. He needed to sell cattle to put more money back into the farm and grow the business. Jemima had enough funds invested to do it ten times over, and that thought made her uncomfortable. When he'd gone to thank her again, all she'd had to do was hold up her hand, and Ned flashed a sheepish grin. One thing she'd make sure of in the coming year was to help out as much as she could without making it too obvious. The girls needed new clothes, and Ryan seemed to grow out of his every time she dressed him.

Jemima had never taken her income for granted, and she'd sought financial advice and invested wisely. She could afford to buy the children some new clothes and some toys for the smaller two. She'd already looked at a couple of horses that Jim Ison was selling but would have to broach the subject with Ned before she bought them.

She slid the two bags off the back of the ute and crossed the yard to the house. The living room was empty as she pushed open the screen door, and she stood there for a minute, uncertain about where to put her bags. She could hear the girls chattering in the bathroom down the hall, and she bit her lip.

A door closed, and Ned walked up the hall. His gaze settled on the two bags.

'Um, where should I put them?' Her voice was hesitant.

Ned walked over and picked them both up. 'In my…our room, I guess.' He lowered his voice. 'I meant to talk to you about this on the way home. We'll have to share a bedroom, but I've figured it out. The last thing we need is for Gwennie to pipe up at school about Daddy's room or Jemmy's room.'

'True. So what are—?'

Ned cut her off. 'Come, and I'll show you what I've planned. Gwennie tells the world everything. I've been trying to teach her what privacy means, but she's a little sharer, and no matter how much I tell her what happens at home is private, it doesn't make a difference.'

'Oh, that could be a problem. We'll have to take care.' She followed Ned across the living room. Jemima hadn't been in the master bedroom before, and surprise filled her when he stood back and let her walk in before him. A massive king-size bed filled the room, and that was it.

There was nothing else in the room. No cupboards, no bedside tables, no clock, not nothing. *Zilch.*

The bed was made, and she could see white sheets at the top beneath the austere grey blanket that looked like an army surplus blanket.

Ned put her bags over near a door at the back of the room. 'There's a wardrobe here that goes through to my bathroom. I don't know if you've seen this section of the house yet?'

Jemima shook her head. 'No, just the kids' bedrooms.'

'So…I think you should take the bed in here, and I've got a small fold-out bed in the walk-in wardrobe. You can go to bed first every night, and I'll come through and sleep in the wardrobe.

If we keep the door locked—'

Ned must have seen the look on her face because he frowned and cut short whatever it was he'd been going to say. 'What's wrong? You have a problem with me sleeping so close?'

'No, of course not. It's not that. You can't lock the door. In fact, you can't shut the door. You won't be able to hear the kids through the night if they get sick or upset or have a dream or something.'

'But if the door's open, they'll be able to see I'm not in the bed.'

Jemima swallowed. Never in a million years had she dreamed she'd say this to a man she barely knew. 'Well then, it's a big bed. You'll have to sleep in it.'

Ned's eyes widened. 'Are you sure?'

Jemima sighed and put more confidence into her voice than she was feeling. 'Look, Ned, I'm not suggesting anything else. It's a huge bed. We've made a deal, and you don't want the idle comment of one of your children to get on the Sykes gossip channel, do you?'

'The what?'

Jemima's tension eased as she laughed. 'The Sykes. Mrs Sykes at the school. Mrs Sykes at the bank and Mrs Sykes at the library.'

Ned's eyes crinkled as he smiled. 'I have no idea what

you're talking about, but it looks like you know the town much better than I do.'

'I'll tell you about them one day, but in the meantime, we need to get organised. If it makes you feel better, we can put a row of pillows in the middle and say I have a bad back or something.'

'Or we could say it was so you can't hear my snoring.'

'What?' This time, Jemima put her hands on her hips as she laughed. 'You snore? That's it! Deal's off.'

'What deal?' came a little quavering voice from the doorway. 'You're not leaving us, too, are you, Jemmy?'

Jemima walked across and kneeled beside Gwennie, whose bottom lip was trembling. 'Oh sweetie, don't be upset. I was just teasing Daddy. He told me he snores.'

'Not very much,' Gwennie said. 'Only when he's very tired.'

Jemima laughed again as she glanced up at Ned. She thought his eyebrows were going to disappear into his hairline.

'But it's okay, Jemmy,' the little girl whispered. 'If it gets too loud, you can come into my bed with me.'

'Thank you. I'll keep that in mind,' Jemima said.

'No, Gwennie, Jemmy will stay in Daddy's bed,' Kelsey said with a wise nod. 'And you know, now that they're married, we all have to give them privacy.'

Ned smiled, and Jemima knew her cheeks were rosy.

'Oh, okay. I get it.' Gwennie turned with innocent eyes, and Jemmy's face grew hotter when Ned grinned at Gwennie's next words, 'So we might get a new baby.'

Kelsey grabbed Gwennie. 'Come on, leave Daddy and Jemmy in peace.'

Jemima put her head down, but Ned didn't let it go. 'I guess there's been some sex education at school. No need to blush.' He ran the back of his hand gently across her cheek.

Jemima couldn't help her smile as she looked up at him. 'Sure sounds like it.'

***

Kelsey was sprawled on the lounge with her iPad in her hand, the light of the screen flickering on her face.

'So, does anyone want any dinner?' Jemima tried to remember what was in the kitchen. It was the thing she was most nervous about—cooking for the family.

'We had dinner at Liam and Angie's before you got home,' Kelsey said.

'And I'm full from the cake,' Gwennie added.

'So it's teeth and bedtime, then.'

Jemima jumped as Ned's breath brushed past her ear, and he put his hand on her shoulder. 'Once the girls are asleep, I'll light the barbie and we can grill some steaks.'

'Oh, there's no need. We had a big lunch, and that cake was

filling.'

'I've got a big day planned tomorrow, so I'll cook myself a steak. You sure you don't want anything?'

'No. I'm fine.' Jemima gestured to the laundry. 'I'll put a load of washing on and then get myself unpacked. At least it's the weekend, and the kids can help around the house tomorrow.'

After the girls went to bed, Jemima kept herself busy. Ned was outside at the grill, and the smell of steak and onions wafted into the house. Her clothes were unpacked—not that she'd brought much with her—the washing was in the basket, ready to hang out in the morning, and the living room was tidy. She walked into the kitchen to put the kettle on for a cup of coffee, but Ned already had it on.

'A coffee?' he asked over his shoulder.

'Yes, please.'

'Pull up a stool. You've not stopped since we got home.'

Jemima waved her hand in the air. 'There's a lot to do. I have to keep up my end of the bargain.'

She held her breath as Ned walked over and pulled up the stool beside her. 'We need to make some ground rules here, Jemmy. I don't expect you to do everything.'

'I don't mind. It keeps me busy.'

'But you're not the housekeeper, and I'm not paying you anything.' He ran a hand through his hair. 'I just appreciate so much what—'

'Enough. I've agreed. The bank's on board, and I don't mind helping out around the house. It's a novelty for me. I've not had to look after anyone apart from me for a long time.'

Ned's smile was rueful. 'You've hit the jackpot with us.'

'Ned!' Jemima shook her head emphatically. 'How many times do I have to tell you that there *is* something in it for me? When I prove that I'm here to stay, and I belong here, and I get a job at the school, I'll be able to say I told you so!'

'I know. But listen, if there's anything you need, just ask. Trust me, okay?' Ned's dark eyes held hers, and those silly nerve endings skittered away again.

'There is one thing,' she said. 'Two, actually.'

'Yep?' He tilted his head to the side.

'I want to buy a couple of horses and put them here on the farm. Kelsey and I can go riding, and we can help you around the place, too.'

'That's fine. As long as you take them with you at the end of the year.'

'Or if Kelsey gets attached, I'll sell you one.'

'Deal.' Ned held his hand out, and Jemima looked at it for a moment before she took his large, calloused hand in hers. She couldn't ignore the spark and couldn't forget that kiss… but this was a business arrangement. Kisses were not a part of that.

'Deal.'

Chapter Twelve

Jemima woke at first light the next morning, but Ned was already gone. She lay back and looked at the ceiling. The farmhouse was old, and there were mould patches in the corner of the bedroom where the ceiling met the cornice. She made a mental note to check the children's bedrooms. It wasn't healthy to sleep in a mouldy room.

She yawned and thought about rolling over and going back to sleep. It had taken her ages to fall asleep once Ned had climbed into the other side of the bed after midnight last night. She'd put the line of pillows down the middle—and felt silly when she did it. She'd worn her watch to bed—as well as a long-sleeved cotton top over her long pyjama bottoms. If she accidentally threw the sheet off in her sleep, at least she'd be decent.

Hot—but decent.

The bed was so big there was room for about six people between them, but it still felt strange sharing a bed with someone she didn't know very well. She'd pretended to be asleep when Ned had said a quiet good night. It had been a long time since Jemima had slept with anyone. She closed her eyes. It had been two years since she'd had a sort-of relationship with one of the photographers in Sydney. And Todd had only stayed with her a couple of nights before he'd moved away to Melbourne anyway.

What if she snored? What if she dribbled in her sleep? Or talked in her sleep? She'd lain there and huffed a sigh as Ned's breathing had evened out within minutes of him getting into bed. He was sound asleep, and yet she'd lain there for ages with her fingers clenched. It would be so easy to roll over and snuggle up against him. Inhale that fresh masculine smell, wrap her arms around his strong shoulders.

Oh God, how many nights was she going to have to lie here and fight the desire coursing through her?

The sound of the fridge door opening brought Jemima awake as she drifted back off to sleep. She swung her legs over the side of the bed and padded into the kitchen.

'Oh, no, you don't, young man.' She swooped down and took the two-litre milk container from Ryan as he tipped it down the sink. Ned had warned her about that happening. He'd solved the mystery of the disappearing milk earlier in the week. Ryan had decided to become independent and get his own cereal. Apparently, it was easier and less messy to tip most of the milk down the kitchen sink before he poured the small portion remaining onto his cereal.

'But I want my cornflakes,' Ryan protested.

'Did you wash your face and hands before you came to the

breakfast table?' Jemima asked sternly.

'No.' The bottom lip wavered.

'Well, come on, and we'll sort you out, and then you can have your cornflakes,' she said confidently.

Cornflakes and milk, she could handle. It was the thought of dinner tonight that had Jemima tied up in knots.

##

The washing was on the line, drying in the end-of-summer sun; the two girls had helped Jemima whip through the house and put things away, and the dishwasher had been run and emptied. She'd found a note in the kitchen from Ned that said:

Will stay out in the paddocks all day. Have packed a feed. See you all at dinner.

Jemima was grateful. Even though she'd been coming over to the house to help out for the past month, she'd only visited for a few hours each day and hadn't done much more than play with Ryan and hang the washing that Ned had done the night before. This was the first time she'd tidied up. Before the wedding, it would have felt like imposing.

'Jemmy, can we unpack some of the boxes in the hall?' Kelsey called out to her after they'd eaten the simple sandwiches she'd managed to make for lunch. 'Daddy has been too busy, and my drawing pencils are in there somewhere.'

'And my Shopkins!' Gwennie added.

'Um, hang on a sec. Just let me finish in the laundry.'

Indecision flitted through Jemima. Should she let the girls into the boxes? Or were they not unpacked for a reason? Ned had been here for a couple of months; maybe there was a reason he hadn't unpacked them.

Or maybe he'd simply been too busy?

For someone who was usually decisive and used to running her own life, Jemima's mind was fraught with indecision. She chewed her lip as she tried to decide, but by the time she came back into the hallway, it was too late anyway. Kelsey was standing on a chair and had the lid of the top box open.

'Be careful. Here, let me.' Jemima helped Kelsey down from the chair. Gwennie was peering into a box at floor level at the other end of the hall. As the little girl pulled out a couple of large packages wrapped in blue tissue paper, Jemima felt uneasy. Her instincts were telling her to close the boxes up and check with Ned first.

Over the noise of the television, where Ryan was firmly ensconced watching cartoons, she heard the creak of the back screen door, and she hurried into the kitchen. Ned was standing at the sink, filling a glass with water.

'Hello. Would you like some lunch?' Jemima looked across to the bread bin. There was just enough bread left for a couple of sandwiches.

'No thanks, I'm fine. I just came in to see if I had an email from Cartwrights. I was waiting for some drench. If it's in, I might have to drive into town.'

'Could we go for you? I could take the kids in for a drive? We need bread.'

'In the Audi?' Ned's grin was broad. 'Sticky fingers and all that.'

Jemima's Audi was in the hay shed where Ned had insisted on covering it with a tarpaulin. The sooner she traded it for something more suitable, the easier it would be.

'Yes, why not? It's a vehicle to get from Point A to Point B. I meant to list it on Gumtree, but I haven't had time.'

'Because…' Ned's voice trailed away.

'Look at me. Look what I found! I'm a princess.' Gwennie stood in the doorway, her little face beaming and a frothy bridal veil trailing to the floor from the top of her head. Jemima's stomach sank, and her mouth dried as Ned's expression closed.

'I told her not to touch it. I told her it was Mummy's.' Kelsey stood behind her.

Ned lifted one hand and then dropped it to his side as he stared at Gwennie.

'I'm sorry, Daddy.' Her bottom lip quivered, and her eyes filled with tears.

'Don't cry, sweetie. I'm sure Daddy thinks you look lovely. Just like your Mummy did.' Jemima walked across to her and crouched down beside her. 'It's a beautiful thing and something that needs to be treasured. How about we take it off and wrap it up carefully and put it somewhere safe?'

Gwennie nodded, and Jemima lifted the white veil from her head.

Ned turned and headed for the office. 'If the drench is in and you could go to town for me, that would be great.' He disappeared down the hall without a backward glance.

Oh, Ned. You should have spoken to Gwennie.

'I didn't . . . didn't'—hiccup—' mean to make Daddy cross.'

Jemima gave the little girl a hug. 'Daddy's not cross. He had to look at something on his computer, that's all. And guess what? We might have to go into town for a drive, and then we can call in and see Lucy and James. How would you like that?'

A wide smile broke through the tears as Gwennie nodded. 'Yes, please!'

'And a milkshake?' Kelsey asked.

'If Con's milk bar is open. I don't know if it will be on a Saturday afternoon.'

'I do miss McDonalds.' Kelsey took the veil from Jemima. 'I'll put this back in the tissue paper. Then where will we put it so it's safe?'

Jemima jumped as Ned's voice came from behind her. 'Put

it on top of the box. I need to get in and unpack the rest.'

She smiled as he ruffled Gwennie's hair on the way past. 'Want to come and feed the chooks with me?' He took Gwennie's hand, and Kelsey and Jemima shared an understanding look that was very mature for an eleven-year-old.

'Daddy did it tough for a while,' she said. 'But now Daddy's got you, things will be right again.'

Guilt trickled through Jemima as she wondered what they'd done. How would the kids cope when she left? They really hadn't thought this scenario through.

***

Ned held Gwennie steady as she stood on the bottom fence railing. They'd fed the chickens, and then she'd decided it was only fair to give Monty a carrot. He still felt guilty for walking out when she'd had Cath's veil on, but he hadn't known what to say. He stared out over Gwennie's head as she held the carrot out to the old horse. Jemima had handled it perfectly. The more he watched the way she was with the kids, the more he was certain that they'd made a good decision.

It was going to help him financially and make the farm viable, but having Jemima leave when the year was up was going to be tough. They would have to plan this better than they had. Ned knew he could be gruff with the kids. He'd been so damn busy trying to be the breadwinner, the housekeeper, and Mummy and

Daddy when they'd lived in Sydney. He knew time for cuddles and affection and one-on-one time with each of them had been short.

Jemima was a natural with them. For someone who'd been in a high-profile international career and had little experience with children, she was unbelievably patient and kind. She had a knack of knowing what to say at the right time. He'd seen her be firm with Ryan when he'd needed it; she was establishing a wonderful rapport with Kelsey through the horses, and Gwennie, sweet little Gwennie, adored Jemmy already. She would make a fabulous teacher when the time came, and he was really lucky that she'd put it on hold and agreed to his plan.

He'd think about it and then talk to her. Maybe he could ramp up the affection with the kids and she could be more the disciplinarian? More aloof, maybe?

No, that was a stupid idea. The kids were responding to the person she was, and anything else would be put on. There was enough subterfuge already.

'Come on, bub. I have to get back to work.' He hoisted Gwennie onto his shoulders, and her giggles made him feel better as he jogged back to the house.

They really needed an exit plan.

***

As soon as Ned checked his email and discovered the drench had arrived at the Cartwright's store, Jemima loaded the kids into the Audi and drove to town. They left the produce store and then called into the grocery store to get bread. A sign on Con's milk bar said, **GONE TO SYDNEY TO VISIT OUR ISABELLA.** There were three smiley emoticons after the words.

'Who's Isabella?' Gwennie asked as the three children stood at the door, disappointment on their faces.

'I don't know, but someone's happy about it. How about we buy some ice cream and flavouring so we can make milkshakes at home?'

The car was full of laughter and chatter on the way home, and she even let the kids share a bag of crisps in the back seat. The Audi could always be cleaned. The kids loved travelling in the sports car, and when she'd mentioned she was thinking of selling it, their cries had howled her down. Maybe she'd keep it for a while longer.

When they got home, there was no sign of Ned or his ute, so they unpacked in the kitchen, and Jemima made milkshakes that Ryan declared were the best ever. Now, the three children were outside playing with Willow. Liam had asked them to babysit the spaniel for the weekend while he and Angie visited the Hunter Valley vineyards.

Jemima's immediate problem was dinner. She opened the small freezer at the top of the fridge, but there was nothing in there that looked familiar or easy. There were always the frozen pre-cooked chicken nuggets and chips—she knew how to heat them, but it couldn't be called a meal. With a sigh, she turned into the hallway, heading for the large laundry room where she knew there were meat packs in the deep freeze. She pulled up short. The hall that had been corded with packing boxes when they left only three hours ago was now empty, and the floor had been swept.

Jemima frowned, wondering what Ned had done with the contents of the boxes. Hopefully, he'd left out the things that the girls had been looking for this morning—Kelsey's pencils and Gwennie's toys. As far as the wedding veil and the wedding dress that had been in the other parcel, it was none of her business where he'd put them. He'd seemed upset, and the fact that he'd cleared the boxes away confirmed that.

Having to tiptoe around someone's feelings was new for Jemima. In the modelling world, she'd seen many tantrums, and the people she'd worked with—both men and women—had been difficult. Models, photographers, agents, stage managers—most had been good, but some had been hard to deal with. She'd learned to remain professional and aloof, so having to contain her feelings here and not get upset about some old boxes and their impact on a family was a totally different world for her. Her chest was tight, and an ache in her throat wouldn't go away.

And then there was dinner. She stood in front of the huge deep freeze in the laundry, staring at the packets of meat. That feeling was now compounded by the dread she held about cooking her first dinner for the family. The tightness in her chest turned into a stone as she stared into the depths of the freezer.

T-bone, eye fillet, brisket, porterhouse, topside, round and chuck? The labels on the meat packets meant nothing to her.

Closing the door, she headed back into the kitchen and picked up her phone to call Lucy, but she remembered Lucy had mentioned that she and Garth were going into town to visit some friends that afternoon. She didn't want to bother her.

'You're all on your lonesome, kid,' she muttered under her breath as she headed back to the freezer. Reaching in, she pulled out the packet that was labelled round steak.

That sounds familiar.

Carrying it into the kitchen, she looked down at the frozen packet. How long was that going to take to thaw out? Even if she cooked some vegetables or made a salad, and Ned cooked the steak on the barbeque, the meat would have to be thawed first. So far, everything had worked out okay, but the thought of putting a meal on the table terrified Jemima. Liam hadn't been joking when he'd teased her about her culinary skills. The only thing she'd ever learned how to cook in Gran's kitchen was pickled onions for the show. The smell of the onions and spices had turned her off cooking for life. After being on the road and living in hotels, room service had been her favourite way to eat.

But there's no room service out here. And no pizza delivery or takeaway shop—in the Outback.

Jemima folded her arms as she stood in the kitchen and surveyed the equipment. She smiled as she spotted the microwave oven. She knew how to use one of them. She'd thaw the meat and then partially fry it up, maybe with some garlic or something and then Ned could take it over to the gas barbeque. If he was late, she'd cook it on the stove, but that would be her last resort. She swallowed and looked at the huge gas contraption that filled one whole wall at the back of the kitchen. When she was bottling onions with Gran one Christmas, she'd heard a bang and turned around to see Gran with singed eyebrows and eyelashes. The gas had backfired. Jemima had been wary of gas stoves ever since.

But the microwave wasn't going to blow up on her. She opened the door, placed the hunk of frozen meat on the glass tray, and shut the door, peering at the digital controls.

Defrost! That's what she needed. She set it for twenty minutes and pressed the power button before going to the small walk-in pantry for some potatoes.

Chapter Thirteen

'Come on, kids, it's past dinner time. Jemmy will be wondering where we are. I thought you'd be starving by now. I am!' Ned walked over to the kids as he came out of the hay shed. He was later finishing than he'd intended—there was always another job to do, but he was enjoying the farm work now that he didn't have to do it all himself. Billy was a godsend, and Ned had learned more about cattle in a week than he'd learned the whole time he'd spent growing up on the property.

'We're still full from our milkshakes,' Kelsey said as she scooped the spaniel under her arm, and Gwennie held out her hand to Ryan—a very grubby Ryan—and they walked across the yard together. The smell of garlic and roasting meat came from the kitchen, and Ned's nose twitched in appreciation.

'Good, all the more for me to eat.' Ned tickled Ryan as he lagged in front of him. Apart from everything else, having Jemima there to cook was going to save him at least an hour every day.

'Come on, buddy, you can come and have a shower with Daddy. I don't know how you manage to get so dirty.' Ned wanted to tidy up for dinner. It was the least he could do to show his appreciation. He was getting way more out of this deal than

Jemima was. 'Girls, you have a wash, too. It smells like dinner's ready.'

Half an hour later, they were sitting at the kitchen table. A small glass jar with rose buds sat in the middle of the table. Jemima had found the red and white checked table mats he'd unpacked earlier, and the cutlery was at each place setting rather than thrown in the middle like it was when the girls set the table when he'd cooked.

Ned frowned when Jemima placed a bowl of salad in the centre of the table and turned back to the cupboard. She was quiet, not saying much as she put the dinner plates on the table. Her brow was furrowed in concentration, and a tiny dimple that he hadn't noticed before appeared in her left cheek when she pursed her lips.

'I think that's everything,' she said as she sat down beside Kelsey. 'Oh, I forgot the potatoes.' She jumped straight back up.

'And the roast,' said Kelsey.

'The roast?' Jemima paused as she lifted the bowl of mashed potato from the benchtop.

'I can smell roast.' Kelsey frowned as she looked at the salad bowl. 'I thought we were having a baked dinner.'

'No. We've got steak and salad, and mashed potatoes, and then peaches and ice cream.' Jemima sounded quite proud as she outlined the menu. 'Oh, and bread. Garlic bread. I almost forgot that.' She went back to the kitchen and opened the oven.

'Do you need a hand?' Ned asked.

'Thanks. I'll get the bread if you can carry the steak for me.'

He left the table and stood behind Jemima as she opened the oven door and slid out a tray of golden bread. She turned with a huge smile and handed him the other oven mitt.

'Perfect. The steaks are on the bottom shelf in that brown dish thing.'

Ned raised his eyebrows.

Brown dish thing? Maybe she casseroled the steak?

'The casserole dish?'

'Yeah, that's it.' Jemima reached up a hand and tucked back a strand of hair that had fallen from her clip. Her cheeks were flushed from the heat of the kitchen, and there was a smudge of something brown on her cheek. He reached over and wiped his thumb gently on her skin.

'Gravy?'

Her flush deepened, and she shook her head. 'No, no, I didn't make gravy. Should I do some?'

'No, I was asking if that was gravy on your face?'

'Shouldn't be.' Her eyes brightened as she smiled back at him. 'Probably dirt off the potatoes when I peeled them.'

'I'm *hungwy*!' Ryan picked up his plate and banged it on the table. Jemima walked over and stood beside him. 'Is that good manners, Ryan?' she asked softly.

'No.' He put his head down and mumbled. 'But you're slower than Daddy.'

Ned carried the casserole dish across to the table and lifted the lid. An overwhelming smell of garlic wafted up, and he frowned as he looked down at the . . . at the . . . something in the dish. It was a sort of grey, but he could see a bit of gristle on the edge. It was definitely meat of some sort, covered with half-cooked onion rings and whole garlic cloves.

'Sit down, Jemmy. I'll serve up.'

Everyone sat quietly as he served each of them a piece of steak and then put the spoon into the potatoes. The yellowish mash stuck to the spoon, and he had to reach for a knife to scrape the glutinous stuff into Ryan's bowl.

'Who'd like some garlic bread? And some salad?' Jemima's voice was louder than usual, and Ned glanced up. Her eyes were wide as she reached hesitantly for the salad bowl.

'Yes, please.' The three kids spoke together as they watched Ned serve their dinner.

Jemima sliced the garlic loaf and then put a piece of bread on each plate. She picked up the salad tongs and placed a slice of tomato and lettuce beside the bread.

Ned sat down. 'You can start now, girls. I'll just cut Ryan's steak for him.' He held the knife firmly as he tried to cut into the steak, but the knife wouldn't go through the plate. All was quiet as everyone watched him try again. Ned looked at the knife and smiled. 'Ah, it's a bread knife. Can you pass me a steak knife, please?'

Jemima passed him a serrated knife, and he tried again. This time, the knife made a tiny tear in the meat.

'Is this meat from the freezer, or did you buy it in town today?' He stopped trying to cut the tough meat and looked over at Jemima. Her face was bright red, and she was blinking quickly.

'From the freezer.'

'What cut is it?' he asked.

What?' she said, brushing the back of her hand over her eyes. 'What do you mean, what cut?'

'Is it rump or—'

'Rump, I think. It started with *R*, anyway. Maybe it's tough because I thawed it out for too long in the microwave. All the juices came out of it.' She rushed on, and her words ran together. 'And then I tried to grill it under the griller, but it went grey, and it curled up. So I put it in the dish in the oven with some water and garlic and onion to make a sort of casserole—what? Why are you all looking at me like that?'

Gwennie and Kelsey were giggling.

'It started with *R*?' Ned said slowly trying to hold back the chuckle that was threatening. 'From memory, I don't think there was any rump left in the big freezer. Maybe it was round steak?'

'Yes, that was it,' Jemima said triumphantly. 'Round steak.'

'And you microwaved it, grilled it, and then casseroled it?' Ned nodded slowly and managed to keep his face serious. 'There must have been something wrong with the beast. After all that attention, it should melt in our mouths.' He couldn't hold back the chuckle any longer and was pleased to see Jemima smile, too.

'So, I stuffed up the first meal I cooked?' She looked over at the girls. 'Don't try and eat it. I'll go find something else.'

'Um . . . do we have to eat the potato stuff?' Kelsey tried to twirl her fork in it and it got stuck.

Ned dug into his and put a forkful in his mouth. 'Yes, it's tasty, and you have to eat your—' Before he could say 'vegetables,' his tongue stuck to the roof of his mouth. He stood and crossed to the sink, tore off a piece of paper towel and tried to spit the offending mass into the towel. Behind him, he could hear the girls giggling as he reached for a glass and turned the tap on.

Finally, he turned around. 'Don't be rude, girls. Jemmy did her best. And that's the lesson we learned from this. Whatever you try, do your best.' He held her gaze and was pleased to see her eyes were dancing.

'The salad is really nice,' Gwennie said quietly.

'Oh, sweetie!' Jemima pushed her chair back, walked around and hugged Gwennie. 'Thank you, but you don't have to eat it.'

'I think we'll find some chicken nuggets and chips in the freezer. How 'bout we show Jemmy how to heat them up in the oven?'

'I already know how to do that,' she said softly. She was still standing next to Gwennie's chair. Ned held his hand out, and she looked at it for a moment.

'Come on, Ms Cosmopolitan. You are about to have your first cooking lesson.'

A slight tingle ran up his arm when Jemmy put her hand in his, and he led her over to the freezer.

##

Two hours later, the children were in bed, their tummies satisfied with oven fries and chicken nuggets. Jemima had gone to bed, and Ned stood beneath the shower for a long time. When she'd taken his hand in the kitchen, a familiar feeling had filled him, but he'd ignored it. That wasn't in the deal; this was a business relationship. He turned the water colder. Taking a cold shower every night for the next year might be hard, but if that's what it took, he was going to have to do it. He stepped out and dried himself before pulling on his boxer shorts and T-shirt. The light was off, and he slipped into bed, pleased to see that the line of pillows was already firmly down the middle.

It took him ages to get to sleep. Jemima wore some sort of

musky body lotion that surrounded him every night. He sat up and turned his pillow over, and then rolled to the very edge of the bed. Maybe he should have insisted they go with his original suggestion. Perhaps the foldout bed in the wardrobe would be safer. He lay there, and finally, Jemima's gentle breathing from the other side of the bed lulled him off to sleep.

The next thing he knew, the bedroom door opened with a creak. Ned struggled out of a deep sleep; it was still pitch dark—a sleep where he'd been dreaming about a soft body pressed close to his.

'Daddy, I'm *firsty.*'

His eyes flew open as Ryan switched on the light. Ned froze. The pillow fence was in a jumbled pile at the foot of the bed, Jemima's head was on his shoulder, and her legs were tangled with his.

He lay there, not sure what to do, but when Ryan ran over to the bed and called out again, 'I'm really *thirsty,*' Jemima opened her eyes, and Ned felt her body stiffen against his as she took a sharp breath.

'It's okay, mate. Daddy will get you a drink.' He lifted his arm, which had somehow gone around her shoulders, and Jemima rolled over and sat up. Her T-shirt was bunched up, and Ned's eyes lingered on her bare stomach before she pulled it down. He had the grace to look away when she glared at him, her cheeks flushed with embarrassment.

'Ah.' Ned cleared his throat as he climbed out of bed. 'Looks like Ryan's a bit unsettled. I'll get him a drink and sleep with him in his bed.'

Jemmy nodded, and it was hard to read the expression on her face.

Disappointment? Embarrassment?

He turned the light off and closed the door as he led Ryan to the kitchen.

Chapter Fourteen

In the next two weeks, a routine developed in the McCormack household. Ned went to bed at midnight each night, waiting until Jemima was asleep before he climbed in on the other side of the pillow wall. Since the night Ryan had woken them up, Ned slept on the far side of the bed and noticed that Jemima did the same on her side. The pillow wall was quickly thrown to the floor each morning when there was a tap on the door, and Gwennie led Ryan in for a morning cuddle so his terror-of-a-son didn't get to the kitchen first and try to get his own breakfast.

As soon as the kids arrived, Jemmy would scooter into the bathroom and leave them to tickles and cuddles. Then, when she came out dressed and ready for the day and took Ryan to the kitchen, Ned would get out of bed.

All very civilised, but what Jemmy didn't know was that he'd lie there listening to her soft breathing until he drifted off to sleep. Sleeping in the same bed as her every night was killing him. She was a beautiful woman, and Ned was discovering more every day that her beauty was way more than skin deep. She was patient with the kids; she was a hard worker—the house was spotless, and the washing and ironing were always up-to-date. Yesterday, he noticed that the gardens inside the house fence had been weeded and watered.

As they cooked dinner together—as they had done since the steak and potato disaster—he looked out into the back garden. There were piles of weeds at regular intervals along the back fence.

'I don't expect you to look after the yard, too, Jemmy.'

'I enjoy that. That's the best part of the day.' Her smile was wide as she stood beside him, peeling the potatoes.

Ned shook his head and moved to stand behind her. He put his arms on either side of her and took the potato peeler from her hand. 'Watch this. If you do it this way, it's much quicker.'

Her hair tickled his nose, and he could feel the warmth of her skin through his work shirt. He stepped back. 'Now you try.'

That wasn't a wise move. He'd have to try and forget how good she smelled before he went to bed tonight.

'Mrs. McGillicuddy rang today.' Jemima's words held a lilt of amusement. 'Apparently, one of your children told them the steak and potato story at school. Mrs. M was there doing volunteer reading.'

'Let me guess. Gwennie's class?' he said with a groan.

'Yes. Anyway, she asked me if I wanted to go to cooking lessons on Friday at the CWA Hall and I think it's a good idea.' Her smile was cheeky now. 'It would save you some time.'

'Only if you want to. We're coping fine now that you've

fessed up about your kitchen skills.' He bumped her with his hip. 'You know, I still would have hired you if you'd told me you didn't cook, although it's hard to believe that a Prickle Creek girl never learned—'

'Hired me? Is that what you call it?' Her chuckle was deep and husky, and unwanted desire slammed through Ned. 'I'll bottle some picked onions next week just to prove you wrong.'

Whoa, boy.

'You didn't hire her, Daddy. You're silly. You married her!' Gwennie was indignant, and Ned and Jemima shared a look of alarm. Desire fled out the window.

'Don't you dare go repeating any more conversations at school, young lady? Or there will be trouble. What is discussed at home stays at home. Is that clear?' Ned kneeled down in front of Gwennie.

'Yes, Daddy.' The tone was meek.

'Don't forget, okay?'

'I won't.'

Ned lifted Gwennie and swung her high. 'Who's the best daddy in the whole world?'

'Um, I don't know.' She giggled as she put her arms around his neck.

Ned pouted. They'd played this game since she was a little girl.

'You are, Daddy!'

'Now give me a kiss, bub.'

'One for me, and then one for Jemmy,' she said with a funny look on her face.

A ripple of alarm ran through Ned. Was Gwennie picking up on the fact that their marriage was not the real thing?

He kissed Gwennie's cheek and put her down. Before he could turn to Jemima, she was at his side and holding her face up.

'My turn.'

Ned smiled and forgot all about Gwennie standing there as he took Jemima into his arms. The kiss she returned was more than a peck on the cheek. He remembered that Gwennie was standing there before he lost control. But when Jemima's lips opened beneath his, he groaned softly and pulled her closer.

Finally, he pulled back and held Jemima's eyes with his. They were half-closed, and the sexy smile on her face sent his blood pressure skyrocketing.

Gwennie patted his arm. 'I like it when you kiss Jemmy, Daddy.'

Ned swallowed and watched as Jemima returned to peeling the vegetables.

'Um, I'll just switch the local news on.' His voice even sounded shaky to him. He followed Gwennie into the living room and tried to focus on the television.

Dinner was quiet, and Ned retreated to his office when the phone rang.

The situation was working out much better than he'd hoped. Jemima had slotted into the household with ease. And she knew the kids so well; she'd been quick to pick up on Gwennie's doubts and had stepped in for that kiss.

The kiss that was going to necessitate another cold shower. He stifled a groan. At this rate, he wasn't going to get any sleep ever. Lying in bed next to Jemima every night with that bloody pillow wall between them was so hard.

The phone rang again, jerking him out of his thoughts.

'Ned, it's Liam. I was wondering if you'd heard about the alliance since you've come home?'

'I've read a little bit about it.' Ned stood, crossed to the window, and pulled the blind down. The outside light had flicked on, and Jemima was at the clothesline hanging the tea towels out.

Jeez, mate. He caught himself staring, and it hadn't even been a full minute since he'd vowed to chop that awareness in the bud.

'We'd love you to join us. If we let them go and do what they're planning, our groundwater will be contaminated right across the Pilliga, and it will affect us all.'

'Sounds good to me. How can I help?'

'I'll let you know when the next meeting's on. We're

making progress. Christos, the company behind it, has just copped a hefty fine for heavy metal contamination of groundwater not far from here.' Liam went on to explain more of the technical details, and before he wound up the call, he warned Ned. 'Keep an eye out. They've been pretty brazen about coming onto farms and doing test drilling. I think Jemmy knows, but just remind her to keep an eye out when you're out on the farm.

'I will. Thanks, mate.' Ned hung the phone up, went back to the window, and put the blinds up. It was dark outside now.

***

Ned wandered out to the kitchen as Jemima turned the dishwasher on.

'Kids in bed already?' he asked.

'Ryan is. The girls are just brushing their teeth.' Jemima folded the dishcloth and placed it on the sink.

'You're doing a great job, Jemmy. I don't think you realise how much you're helping. Getting things back to normal, and I'm spending so much more time with the kids. It's been a long time for us.'

A rush of affection for this man ran through her. 'It's not all my doing'—she put one hand up—'don't you dare say thank you.'

'I'll go and tuck the kids in. Can you come to the office in a while? I want to have a bit of a chat.'

'A chat?'

'Nothing bad. I just want to streamline some of the points of our agreement.'

'Oh, okay. I'll put the kettle on, and we can have our cuppa in there. Is that okay?'

Ned nodded and disappeared down the hall, and Jemima put her hand to her chest, worrying that she'd done something to upset Ned.

A few minutes later, she carried a tray with a pot of coffee and a plate of homemade biscuits that she'd made at the CWA last Friday. She was quite proud of them. Ned came in and closed the door.

Jemima poured the coffee and passed him the plate. 'A Melting Moment? Homemade.' She beamed.

Ned took a bite and nodded. 'Pretty good.'

Jemima sat back in the chair and sipped her coffee. 'So, what's wrong? Have I stuffed up somewhere?'

'No, not at all. I think things are going really well. Brilliantly, in fact. The farm is going so much better than I thought it would this early on. Meeting up with Liam and Garth has been the best thing for the farm—I've got a business plan in place since the bank loan came through, plus the line of credit at the produce store makes it easy to do the accounts. And Billy, he's the farmhand that everyone would love to have.'

'So?'

Ned leaned forward and dropped his head into his hands. 'Some things are going too well.'

'Oh, like what?' Jemima bit her lip. *What is coming?*

'The kids.'

'How can they be going too well?'

Ned looked up and held her gaze. 'You are so good with them. You know when to praise, and you know when to be firm, and I appreciate it very much.'

'I don't understand why there's a problem. I love looking after them, and I love spending time with them.' Jemima smiled and tried to lighten the atmosphere that was quite tense. 'Even playing with Ryan and his little cars in the dirt. Not to mention hide-and-go-seek.' But the memory of playing hide-and-seek didn't change his expression.

'That's the problem. They love you.'

'Oh? That's a problem?'

Ned reached over and took her hand. Jemima looked down at his tanned fingers holding hers.

'You're such a good person, and you've taken family life on board so well. Never in my wildest dreams did I think it would work so well, even after only a couple of months. We're all settled and happy. Happier than I ever thought would be possible again.'

'That's good,' she said softly.

'I want to ask you something.' Ned's gaze locked with hers, and Jemima's breath stilled.

Surely not? Surely he wasn't going to suggest that they make this a real marriage? Confusion swirled through her. What would she say? What did she think about that? She stared down at his hand, and she knew that she'd agree in a heartbeat. Not only did she love his children, but her feelings for Ned McCormack confused her. Since the afternoon they'd played hide-and-seek with Ryan and Ned had kissed her in the linen cupboard, she'd tried hard to keep her feelings on a platonic level.

But it was hard, and Jemima knew she was fighting a losing battle. *Maybe I won't have to fight it anymore.* A little tendril of hope took root in her heart.

Self-protection. It was the first time in many years that she'd been accepted for who she was and not what she looked like.

'What did you want to ask me, Ned?' His brown eyes were dark and shadowed, and she squeezed his hand when his eyebrows lowered in a frown. 'Don't be scared to say what you think.'

'Good. I was worried how you'd take it.'

Jemima bit her lip as she waited. Her heart beat hitched up a notch as that tendril grew a little bit more.

'I want you to help me with an exit plan.'

'A what?' Her fairytale dreams flew out the window at his brisk tone, and the little tendril of hope withered.

'An exit plan.' Ned let go of her hand and fired up the computer. 'I noted down some ideas when I was in here the other night.'

'Yes?' Jemima folded her arms.

'When the year is up, the kids are going to be upset.' The shadows deepened in his eyes and she resisted the urge to reach out and take his hand back. 'They've already suffered enough loss in their lives, and I don't want it to be so hard when you leave.'

'Fair enough. So what is this exit plan?'

Ned turned and looked at the computer screen, and Jemima looked past his shoulder. There was a list of bulleted dot points, but the font was too small for her to read.

Ned swivelled back around on his chair.

'I think that the affection needs to stay with me. If you pretend that you're their school teacher, even though you're living here twenty-four seven, it should be easy to remember.'

'I don't understand what you're saying. Affection stays with you?'

'Yes, aren't there rules for how much a teacher can touch a child these days?'

Jemima nodded. 'Yes, of course there are.'

'So, if you stick to those types of rules—after all, since this is just a job to you—I'll give the cuddles and the kisses, and the kids will come to me more. Hopefully, they'll see you more as the one who looks after their practical needs.'

Jemima could sense what he was saying, but it wasn't going to be easy. 'I can do that, but don't you think they might wonder why I don't cuddle them anymore? I'm supposed to be their new mother, Ned.'

'I know. I've thought of nothing else for the past few days. But I think it's the only way we can do this. Will you try?'

'Of course, I will. After all, you're the one who's calling the shots here. And you're the one who'll be left with the mess at the end of the year.' Jemima drained her coffee cup. 'If that's all, I have some things to do.'

Ned caught her hand as she reached for the tray. 'I don't expect you to work so hard, you know. I think we've got through the hardest part and convinced everyone.'

Jemima managed to summon up a smile as bitterness tainted her stomach. 'Yes, I think we have.'

But she disagreed that they'd got through the hardest part. There were still nine months to go.

Chapter Fifteen

The following month passed quickly. Ned and Jemima had been married for almost four months, and the farm was looking good. The wheat was growing, and the cattle were fattening quickly. The girls had settled into school and were making friends, and their second term at Prickle Creek School was beginning. Autumn was moving into winter with its misty and cool mornings, and Ned had started to light the wood fire at night. Ryan had started at the preschool, and Jemmy was still going to the CWA hall for cooking lessons each Friday, much to the amusement of the CWA ladies. The meals at the farm over the past weeks, if not gourmet quality, had been tasty, nourishing and edible—at least.

And filling. Ned hadn't complained, and the kids had actually started to clear their plates each night.

That *was* satisfying.

The only thing that was bothering her was sharing a bed with Ned each night.

That *wasn't* satisfying.

Since the night she'd somehow breached the pillow wall and wrapped herself around him—heat still flushed into her cheeks every time she thought about it—she was so conscious of staying on her side of the bed that she woke herself up about ten times each night, checking that she was still on her side. They'd never mentioned it after Ned had taken Ryan out for a drink that night.

And, of course, Lucy was right onto Jemima.

'So, are you sharing a bed?'

Ned had gone to town with Liam for an alliance meeting, and he'd dropped Jemima and the three children over at Lucy's house for her famous pizza. He was going to call in and collect them on his way home. The two women watched as darkness stole over the paddocks outside. Jemima felt the blush run up her neck and into her cheeks as her cousin stared at her. Lucy had poured them each a wine, and they were sitting on the enclosed back porch watching another spectacular sunset. Garth was too busy to go to the meeting, and he was engrossed in farm accounts in his office. James was on his play mat; the only sound was his occasional *goo*. So, a perfect time for girl talk, according to Lucy.

'Yes . . . we sleep in the same bedroom.'

'You know what I mean. Are you sleeping together?'

'Yes, I sleep, and he sleeps.'

'Jeez, Jemmy! Do I have to spell it out?' Lucy's eyes were sparkling with naughtiness. Give her wine, and she always got too personal. 'Have you done the deed?'

'What?' Jemima burst out laughing. 'You sound like you did when you were sixteen and first falling for Garth. But no—not that it's any of your business— we haven't "done the deed" as you so rudely ask.' She shook her head and sipped her wine as the kids' voices drifted in from the spare bedroom where they were watching a movie. 'And we won't.'

'Why not? He's a red-blooded man, and you have a need, don't you?'

'Honestly, Lucy. You're awful when you drink wine. I thought you were off it while you were breastfeeding?'

'James is half on the bottle now, so I can have the occasional wine. I couldn't keep up with him, hungry little man.' Lucy reached down and ran her fingers over the baby's downy head.

'He's certainly growing.' Jemima looked over at her chubby nephew lying on a colourful play mat.

'So?' Lucy tipped her head to the side.

'So what?'

'You have needs, don't you?'

'Really, Lucy! Well, yes, of course I do. But that's not part of the deal.'

'What would it hurt? Have you talked about it?'

'No, we haven't mentioned it. Jeez, Lucy, I feel disloyal to Ned talking about this.'

'Why? He's not your husband?'

'He is, legally.'

'But he's not really your husband, especially if you're not having sex. I don't think you guys thought this through well enough.'

'*Ssh*. Keep your voice down.' Jemima swallowed. Not because she was embarrassed by Lucy's suggestion but because she'd lain in the same bedroom as Ned last night, thinking the same thing. Lucy had just put her thoughts into words. 'I don't want Garth to hear.'

'He won't hear. He's absorbed in his cattle prices. How a man can sit there for hours and look at weights and figures, I'll never know.'

'It's your livelihood.' Jemima was pleased that Lucy had got off the subject of her sex life, but the relief was short-lived.

'So, you're skirting around it?'

'No, we haven't even discussed it.' Jemima frowned. Lying in bed next to Ned with the pillow fence between them, wondering what it would be like to snuggle up against him—and more— didn't count as discussion.

'Do you find him attractive?' Her cousin wasn't going to drop it.

'Of course I do! He's a fine-looking man, and he's a *good* man. I like him, and I respect him.'

'And you lust after him, too?' Lucy said with a giggle.

'*Lucy!*' Jemima looked around, but Garth wasn't interested

in their conversation. He was focused on his computer screen.

'So, what are you going to do about it?'

'Nothing. There's nothing to discuss.' Jemima put her wine glass on the coffee table and leaned back in the chair. 'I don't know why we're even having this conversation.'

'It's not natural, you know.'

'Lucy, for God's sake. His wife died, and I'm looking after his kids. I'm the nanny or the governess, whatever tag suits the role. It's not that sort of relationship. In fact, there's no relationship. There was never going to be. It's business, pure and simple. I'm helping Ned, and I'm getting experience towards my teaching. He said he'd give me a great reference at the end of the year. Even if I don't get a job at the school, there are always plenty of governess positions advertised. I've looked in *The Land*.'

'Not the sort you want.' Lucy smiled over the rim of her wine glass.

'No more,' Jemima said, holding up her hand. 'Can we talk about something else? The kids are occupied, and I was hoping for a bit of downtime. Being a housekeeper and nanny, helping with homework, and learning to cook and shop is heavy going. Not to mention all the emotional stuff that goes with being part of a family household.'

Trying not to be affectionate with the kids was doing Jemima's head in. She had to think every minute of the day.

'Not for much longer, sweetheart.'

'What's not for much longer?'

'Your downtime. Here comes the good-looking guy that you're sleeping with but not sleeping with.' Lucy's smile spoke volumes.

'Lucy,' Jemima hissed. 'For goodness' sake, keep your voice down and get that secret smile off your face. That's the last time I'm drinking wine with you. Now behave!'

Jemima jumped up, hurried across the living room, and opened the front door before Lucy could get out of her chair.

'Hi Ned. Come in. Good meeting?' She glanced over at Lucy and shook her head as she mouthed to her, *Be good.*

Garth looked up from the computer through his open office door. 'Ah, at last, Ned. You can save me from a chick-talk-slow-and-painful death.'

Jemima froze and glared at Lucy again as Ned chuckled and crossed the room to the door of Garth's office.

'How did the meeting go, mate? Sorry I couldn't make it tonight, but I'm way behind on my records.' Garth turned the screen off and stepped into the living room. 'Can I offer you a beer?'

'No thanks, but I'd love a cuppa and some leftover pizza if there's any. Where are the kids?'

'I'm assuming they're all asleep in the spare room,' Garth

said with a glance at Lucy and Jemima. 'Curled up in the king-size bed. They wore themselves out.'

Lucy nodded. 'They gorged on pizza and then played with James. We haven't heard a peep since we put *Moana* on.'

'I thought that might be the case. I parked near the front door.'

'Jemmy, why don't you leave them here for the night? Shame to wake them up. Go home with Ned, and you can get the kids tomorrow,' Lucy said brightly.

Jemima gritted her teeth and tried to glare at her cousin, but Ned was blocking her view. 'I could sleep here, too, on the fold-out lounge, if the kids stay,' she said.

Ned walked across to the kitchen with Garth. 'That's a good idea, Lucy. I'd appreciate it.'

Jemima felt as though her eyes were on stalks like those cartoon characters that Ryan was always watching, but her surprise eased as Ned kept talking. 'Because I could use an extra hand in the morning cutting those cattle out. If the kids stay here, you could help.'

Jemima flashed a triumphant look at Lucy. *See! Sex is the last thing on Ned's mind.*

Although it did hurt a little bit in a place she kept hidden away from the world. She'd discovered that men merely viewed her as a conquest. Knowing she was simply a trophy on someone's arm had put a huge dent in her self-confidence.

Okay, so I was lucky enough to be born with good looks. No one ever wanted to get to know the real Jemima Smythe. And Ned was no different. He wasn't attracted to her at all. If he had been, surely she would have picked up some sort of vibe, sharing a bed with him over the past few months? No, she was purely and simply someone to look after his kids. Even though she'd agreed to the arrangement, she'd been relegated to about fifteenth place in his priorities.

And it hurt. Just a little bit, and it didn't do a lot for her self-esteem.

Where did she sit in the scheme of things?

After the kids, of course. That she understood. He was their dad, and they'd always come first. Heck, she was just the nanny, and she loved the three of them even though she couldn't hug them.

Which was so hard.

Jemima pushed away the thought of leaving Kelsey, Gwennie, and Ryan at the end of the year.

After the cattle, well, okay, that was his livelihood and the whole point of their deal. If it wasn't for the farm, he wouldn't have needed the bank loan, and he wouldn't have needed her.

After the wheat fields, he'd just sown. That had been her suggestion. And one that Ned had really appreciated. That was the night he'd lifted her and swung her around as the kids cheered. *Go, Dad!*

And she probably came after the new litter of the kittens in the hay shed, too.

Oh, for goodness' sake, stop feeling so sorry for yourself.

'You could always do something about it.' Lucy's words buzzed around Jemima's head as she sat there listening to Ned fill Garth in on the alliance meeting.

***

Ned stood in Lucy's kitchen sipping his tea and looked over at Jemima. Her hair was loose—he loved it when she wore it out, and that wasn't often enough. She was wearing some sort of casual floaty pants, and her legs were tucked up beneath her, and a glass of wine dangled from her fingers. The fitted T-shirt accentuated her breasts, and he found it hard to look away. She'd put something around her eyes and her lips tonight, and she was even more stunning than usual.

Which was stunning enough without any enhancements.

Ned cleared his throat as she lifted a languid gaze to his, and for a moment, he could have sworn he saw his need reflected in her expression. But it was gone before he could blink. Of course, she wanted to come home and have a good night's sleep. The last few weeks, the shadows had deepened beneath Jemima's eyes, and he was worried she was working too hard. What if it became too much for her and she realised she wanted to go back to the city? He'd be caught between a rock and a hard place if that happened.

With the kids not there tonight, there was no need to keep up appearances. He could sleep in Ryan's bed, and Jemima could get a good night's sleep. God knew he needed one. Lying next to her in that king-size bed every night was torture. A couple of nights ago he'd finally gone to sleep with his fingers clenching the sheet so he didn't reach over and hold her. He tried not to think about it.

What man wouldn't be the same with a woman as beautiful as Jemima in bed next to him?

It didn't mean anything.

Lucy yawned and broke into Ned's thoughts. 'I'm going to bed. Jemmy, if you do decide to sleep on the cane lounge, there's a spare blanket in the cupboard in the hallway. If you're going home, I'll feed the kids in the morning.'

'Have you got Weetbix?' Ned and Jemima spoke together, and he looked at her and laughed.

'Yes, I do. Now get off home,' Lucy said. 'I'm going to bed before James wakes up for his next feed.'

Lucy padded softly down the hallway.

'Well?' Ned raised his eyebrows. 'Coming or staying?'

His mouth dried as she pushed herself to her feet. Almost six feet of a perfect figure unwound sinuously as she stood. She stretched, and that damned T-shirt clung even tighter.

'I'll come home,' she said, 'and help with the cattle.'

He hid the smile that tugged at his lips, unsure of why he felt so pleased that she wanted to come home with him. Or maybe it was simply because she called it home.

It wasn't just the help she would give him with the cattle work. The thought of going home to an empty house hadn't appealed.

But on the other hand, the thought of going home with Jemima and no children appealed way too much.

'Night, Garth.'

'See you tomorrow.'

Garth's eyebrows rose as Jemima turned to the door, and damn if he didn't wink at Ned.

Ned frowned and shrugged as though he didn't understand. He followed Jemima to the door. He held open the car door for Jemima as she climbed up into the ute. When he was in the driver's seat and had started the car, she yawned again.

'Sorry. I should know better than to drink wine. But don't worry, I only had two glasses. I was keeping an eye on the kids. I checked on them just before you came in. The three of them were sound asleep in the king bed. And Ryan took his Teddy, so he's happy.'

'It's okay, Jemmy. You don't have to explain yourself.

You're entitled to some downtime. You work too hard.'

He flicked a sideways glance at her. For once, he wished he could find the courage to say what he really wanted instead of being polite and keeping a distance between them. To tell her that not only was he happy with the way she looked after his kids, the way she kept the house and looked after everything to free him up for the farm work, and the way she was learning to cook for them. He'd like to be able to be honest, for once. He liked having her in the house just because of who she was.

He liked her. Too much.

But he couldn't tell Jemima the truth. If he told her how bloody hard it was lying so close to her in that bed every night and how he dreamed of running his fingers over her soft skin, it would ruin everything. They had a business relationship, and he liked to think they were slowly developing a friendship, and trust was too big a part of that for him to blow it by telling her what he was thinking most nights.

Besides, it would only be sex. There was no future. He wasn't looking for a real marriage. He wasn't going to risk his heart again. And despite what she said, he still couldn't believe that she really wanted to stay out here in the Outback when the year was up.

Chapter Sixteen

As they walked into the house, Ned flicked the living room light on.

'There's no need to get up at the crack of dawn. If we can get out in the paddock by eight, that'll give us plenty of time before we pick up the kids.'

'And an opportunity to sleep in without having to worry about Ryan getting into the cereal and milk before we wake up.' As Jemima spoke, a soft pink blush stained her cheeks. The way she'd said "before we wake up" sounded intimate, and it obviously bothered her.

She put her bag down on the coffee table and headed towards the hall. 'I'm going to have a shower.'

Five minutes later, Ned shut the door to his office and flopped into the chair. He could hear the shower running in the bathroom down the hall, so he turned the computer on, but trying to focus on cattle weights and calf numbers rather than thinking of Jemima in the bathroom under the shower didn't work, so he gave up.

With a groan, he turned the computer off and dropped his head in his hands.

What the hell is the matter with me? What am I doing?

Jemima would be gone at the end of the year. He didn't need her in his life past that. He didn't want her in his life. He didn't. He'd sworn to himself he'd never get married again—he'd never replace Cath. He couldn't go through that grief again. He and the kids had been sort of happy before Jemima came. She was there mainly to take over the house chores and the day-to-day kid stuff. And not to forget the main reason. To provide the security for the loan that had let him hire Billy. The property was already well and truly getting in the black, and he was able to spend much more time with his kids.

And Jemima.

In the first quarter, he'd paid almost half of the loan back. Cattle prices were high, and he'd have it sorted by the end of the year.

Being attracted to Jemima was natural. Two adults living in close proximity—they should have realised it would happen. When she left, this need that consumed him would disappear.

***

Jemima switched the shower off and reached for the towel. As she wiped her face, she took a deep breath.

Why had she come home with Ned?

It had been stupid, and if it hadn't been for the wine, she would have thought rationally.

For a moment, she let herself dream that he had an ulterior motive—that he'd wanted her here without the kids and then she let out a bitter laugh.

That was *her* dream.

To Ned, she was the nanny, the housekeeper, and the occasional farmhand.

And the security for his loan. Nothing more, nothing less. If he knew that she was fighting falling for him with every fibre of her being, he'd have her out of his house like a shot, and she couldn't bear that. How she was going to leave at the end of the year was something she couldn't even think about. She was devising her own 'exit plan,' thinking about her future when she left the McCormacks. It would be wise to go back to Sydney, as much as she didn't want to. She'd have a much better chance of getting a job in the many schools there compared to Prickle Creek, where the local school was the only one for about one hundred kilometres. Yep, that's what she'd do. See the contract out, look after the kids, and try to keep her heart whole.

As she opened the bathroom, a sliver of light shone under the office door. Jemima closed the bathroom door soundlessly and tiptoed down the hall, wrapped in a towel. All of her clothes were in the master bedroom, and she'd been so caught up in her thoughts she hadn't collected them before she'd gone to the kids' bathroom.

She opened the door quietly and walked across to the walk-in wardrobe that she shared with Ned. She shook her head. There was no way that the kids would slip up and tell anyone about the marriage being a fake. The only thing that didn't make it a true marriage was what Lucy had been talking about. *Sex.*

Jemima stood on her toes, and as she reached the top shelf for her PJs, the towel slipped off. In the same instant, the door to the ensuite opened, and the wardrobe was bathed in bright light. She screamed and grabbed for the towel on the floor. Ned stood there, and he looked as shocked as she had felt. As she bent down for her towel, she realised he was as naked as she was.

'Oh, God, sorry.' Ned reached behind for what she assumed was a towel as she held hers in front of her. Jemima didn't know where to look, so she focused on the light above the door.

'I thought you were in the study,' she said.

'I couldn't concentrate.' Ned's voice sounded funny, and he wouldn't meet her eyes, even though they were both decent now—or as decent as you could be with only a towel around you.

'I thought I'd have a quick shower and get out of here before you went to bed.'

'This is your bedroom. I can sleep in one of the kids' beds.' Jemima was fixed to the spot, but she knew she had to move so Ned could walk through to get out of the bathroom. He seemed as reluctant to move as she did, and when she finally dropped her eyes from the light, he had the strangest look on his face.

'No, no. That's fine. You take the big bed.' He cleared his throat as though he was coming down with something. She frowned. He had twin spots of red on his cheekbones.

'You're not getting sick, are you?' She clutched the towel tightly around her with her fist walked over, and put her other hand on Ned's forehead.

'*Hmm*, you are a bit warm.' As she spoke, a strangled sound came from his throat.

'What's wrong? Is your throat sore?'

Ned clutched the towel to his waist and reached out with his other hand. For a moment, he simply held her hand and stared at her. Jemima's heart set up a thunderous beating, and she closed her eyes, wanting to break that look of intimacy they were sharing. She had as much chance of keeping the desire from her expression as she did of whipping up a gourmet meal.

But it was too late. Inch by inch, Ned pulled her closer until she could barely breathe. It was impossible not to move towards him as his hand tugged her closer. His arm went around her, and when his body touched hers, Jemima whimpered softly. Little tingles ran through every nerve ending in her body when his slightly damp but warm chest pressed against her bare skin. The tingles turned the warmth to fire, and she opened her eyes.

She had to know that Ned was feeling the same as she was, although the evidence was certainly there as he pressed against her.

'What are you doing?' she whispered, holding his gaze. His eyes were a deep brown, and she was close enough to see the golden flecks in the centre of each iris. His breath moved her hair, and the smell of lemon soap surrounded them. Jemima let out a sigh as the heat from his skin warmed her all over. The feel of his muscular thighs against her legs sent another rush of desire coursing through her.

'Do you think it would be silly if we slept in the same bed?' Ned dropped his forehead to hers.

'Do you?'

'No.'

'Me neither.'

'Without the pillows?' His breath puffed on her face as his lips hovered above her cheek.

'Without the pillows would be good.' Jemima nodded, and heat ran to her face. Her towel slipped to the floor. She closed her eyes as Ned let go of his towel, too. His fingers held her chin lightly, and he tipped her head up. His lips touched hers so gently she wasn't even sure if she could feel them.

'Um, I just have to go to the high cupboard in the kitchen,' he said.

'High cupboard?'

'Where the medical stuff is.' His lips tilted against hers in a smile. 'As long as they're not out of date.'

Jemima frowned and then realised he was talking about protection. 'It's okay. I'm on the pill.' With a sigh, she opened her lips and relished the strength of his arms as he lifted her.

As though he'll never let me go.

She held his gaze as he carried her across to the bed and laid her gently on the soft sheets. She held his gaze as Ned lay beside her. He sighed and trailed his fingers over her face.

'You are so beautiful, Jemmy.'

His fingers moved down to her neck and lingered on her shoulders, and she took a breath as they moved down ever so slowly.

The pillow fence wasn't built or missed that night.

In the hour before dawn, as the sky lightened outside and the mournful call of a beast echoed through the misty paddocks, Jemima lay next to Ned, nestled against his warmth, listening to his deep breathing. The number of nights she'd lain next to him over the past months, she'd never heard that deep and contented sound before. Maybe he'd lain awake like she had.

Whatever it had been, things had changed, and she wasn't sure what would happen now. But she wasn't going to worry about it.

A girl could dream.

Chapter Seventeen

Waking up in the same bed she'd slept in for the last three months was very different this morning. Jemima rolled over, but the other side of the bed was empty. She didn't know whether to be pleased or sad. She buried her face in Ned's pillow and inhaled the fresh lemon smell that lingered on the pillowcase before she glanced at the bedside clock that she'd placed on the bedside table that she'd brought over from her room at Gran's farm.

Seven thirty! Boy, had she overslept. Ned was probably out with the cattle already, and here she was, sleeping-in. She tore out of bed, jumped in the shower, dried herself quickly, threw on a pair of riding pants and a long-sleeved shirt, and grabbed a sleeveless fleece vest.

An amused voice came from the kitchen as she ran through the living room, pulling her damp hair into a ponytail.

'Where's the fire?'

She pulled up in her tracks and turned slowly before she walked into the kitchen. Ned was standing against the sink, nursing a cup of coffee. His hair was still wet, and he was wearing his work clothes.

God, she hated the morning after, but this morning's

scenario was way out of her experience. Jemima was used to being in control of her life and the occasional night with a sophisticated person who knew that the relationship was only for the short term. This was the man she was living with. And was married to, for goodness' sake.

'Um, no. I thought you'd gone out to the paddocks already.'

'Slow down, there's no rush. I rang Lucy, and she's going to keep the kids there till lunchtime. She said they'd turn the barbeque on about noon.'

'What did you tell her?' Jemima gulped.

'I said that we were just in for a cuppa and that there was a bit more to do than I'd realised.' Jemima's legs trembled as Ned laughed and walked over to her. 'Lucy didn't need to know we haven't been out to the cattle yet.' His arms went around her, and he dropped a kiss on the top of her head. 'So, what are we going to do now?'

'Cut the cattle out?' Her grin was cheeky.

'No. Us. We can't get an annulment now.'

Jemima laughed. 'Not now we've done the deed.' She was pushing logic away and enjoying the light and free feeling that had been with her since she'd woken up.

'What? The deed?' His grin was wide, and her stomach curled again. He was such a good-looking man, and it was wonderful to see him smile.

'Nothing. Girl joke.'

'Anyway, seeing you had a lie in, we'd better hurry up and get out to these cattle. Do you want a quick cup of coffee?'

'No, thanks. I'll just take some water out there.' She wasn't going to tell him that her stomach was churning with nerves. They would have to get a divorce, not an annulment. Ned would have to work it out. She put her hand on her tummy, and it gave a funny little flip.

##

By the time they'd moved most of the cattle, Jemima knew that her stomach wasn't churning because of any desire to be back in the bedroom with Ned, or any worry about annulments or divorces. Unfortunately, it was a bathroom that she needed. A wave of cold washed over her, and she shivered, but at the same time, a trickle of perspiration ran down her neck. She pulled the water bottle from the saddle and almost gagged, and her stomach rumbled. All she could taste was pineapple.

'Are you okay?' Ned frowned as he brought his horse close to hers. 'You're very pale.'

'I do feel a bit sick,' Jemima said as her cheeks heated with embarrassment. 'I think I've eaten something that's disagreed with me.'

'Head back to the house. I'll be finished here in less than half an hour.'

'Thanks, I'm sorry to let you down.' She gave him a weak smile and pulled Monty's reins to turn back to the house.

By the time she'd dismounted, put Monty away, and made it to the house, her stomach was really hurting. Jemima put her hand against it and headed for the bathroom, but the phone trilled in the kitchen.

For a second, she thought of ignoring it, but as she glanced at the digital display, Lucy's name flashed up.

'Hello.' Her voice was weak, and her head spun as she picked up the phone.

'Jemmy? I just rang to see if you and Ned are okay. I think something on the pizzas must have been off. Everyone over here is sick—except me.'

'Oh, no.' Jemima straightened. 'How bad are the kids?'

'They're okay now. They each had a vomit. I gave them a bath, and the three of them are asleep now. Poor little Ryan was crying for Ned.'

'I'll send him over as soon as he gets back in. And Lucy, it was the pineapple. It's all I can taste. Oh no, I have to run.' She threw the phone down and ran for the bathroom.

***

As it turned out, Ned and Lucy were the only ones who hadn't eaten the ham and pineapple pizza. Lucy was full of apologies when Ned went across to pick up Kelsey, Gwennie, and Ryan.

'Daddy!' His little boy snuggled into him. 'I was sick. Two times.'

'I'm so sorry, Ned. That pineapple must have been in the freezer for longer than I'd thought.' Lucy frowned as she held Kelsey and Gwennie's hands.

'Don't worry. Everyone's okay now.'

'What about Jemmy?'

'She's asleep. She managed to get a cup of tea down and went back to bed.' Ned opened the car door and strapped Ryan into his seat. 'Come on, girls. We'll get you home.'

'Oh, I feel so bad.' Lucy put her hand to her mouth, and Ned walked over to hug her.

'Don't be silly. These things happen.' He grinned at her. 'But we might give pizza a miss for a while.'

Kelsey and Gwennie chattered as they drove the short distance through the back gate of Garth and Lucy's farm, via the shortcut via Prickle Creek Farm and then across the road to Daniela.

'Daddy, why did Grandpa call the farm, Daniela?' Gwennie asked as they drove through the front gate. Amazing how quickly kids bounced back; poor Garth was still in bed, like Jemmy.

'I don't know. We'll have to ask him next time they ring up.'

'Maybe Nanny and Grandpa could come up for another

visit,' Gwennie suggested.

'Maybe,' Ned agreed. But he wasn't really keen on the idea. He knew his parents would love Jemima. It would be better to keep them away until she'd left. So many damn complications had surfaced that he hadn't even thought of when he'd come up with this plan.

Not least their sleeping together last night. In the afterglow after last night, he'd joked about not being able to get an annulment, but sleeping with Jemima had caused a problem. Now, they'd have to divorce.

'Where's Jemmy?' Kelsey asked as though she'd read his mind.

'She's lying down. I want you all to be quiet when we go inside in case she's still asleep.'

'Poor Jemmy,' Gwennie said. 'I hope she's all right. Daddy, I do love her.'

Ned froze as his daughter's voice came over the seat. His stomach clenched, and for a minute, he wondered if he was getting sick, too. But he knew it was Gwennie's words that had done it. *I do love her.*

Ned's hands gripped the steering wheel.

What have I done?

Sleeping with Jemima last night had been foolish and unfair to her when he had no intention of making this a permanent relationship. He couldn't afford to get emotionally tied to her, and after last night, he was going to have to fight that very thing.

Gwennie's words wouldn't leave him as he drove towards the homestead. *I do love her.* So much for his "exit strategy" of Jemmy not being affectionate with the kids. That obviously hadn't worked.

Ned stifled a groan. What the heck was he going to do? He'd stuffed things up well and truly. The happiness and contentment that had filled him this morning when he'd woken up beside Jemmy was replaced by regret and worry. The farm was going well, but the means he'd used to get there was going to cause a lot more complications than he'd ever considered.

How the hell was he going to talk to Jemima about it?

Thanks for a good night, but we won't do that again.

Or would he just say nothing and keep his distance? No, that was cowardly.

Ned sighed as he pulled up to the shed.

'What's wrong, Daddy? Are you worried about Jemmy, too? Maybe we can take her a cup of tea?' Gwennie reached over to him as she unclipped her seatbelt.

'We'll see, bub.'

They crept into the house, but the bedroom door was closed. Ned put his fingers up to his lips and pointed to the living room. The three children—still a little bit pale—didn't argue. Ned opened the bedroom door a crack. Jemima was fast asleep, one hand curled beneath her cheek. He ignored the funny feeling that settled in his chest as he headed to the kitchen to prepare a light dinner for his children.

Chapter Eighteen

Ned ran his hand down Monty's smooth nose and chuckled. 'You're a smart old thing.' He shut the gate, walked into the hay shed, and dug in the hessian sack for a carrot. The last time Jemima had gone into town, she'd brought home a bag of carrots from the produce store, and Monty was getting spoiled by everyone.

'A carrot a day is good for his teeth,' Kelsey had informed him knowledgeably yesterday after she'd gotten off the school bus. The horse paddock was her first stop, and he'd just put Monty in there.

'What about ten a day?' Ned had ruffled her hair. 'Is that ten times better?'

Kelsey had shot him one of her 'oh really, Dad' looks and had dug out another carrot for Monty.

'And spoiled.' He gave him a last pat and crossed the yard to the house. He'd finished earlier than he'd expected down at the back paddock, where the new cattle were contently filling their stomachs. And growing fatter.

The only downside was the tension between him and Jemima. Since the night they'd spent together, he knew she was confused by the distance he was keeping. It was the best thing for both of them. The couple of times he'd tried to start a conversation with her about it, she'd fobbed him off.

Maybe this was a good time to talk. The girls were at school, and Ryan was at preschool. He knew that he'd hurt Jemima with his aloof attitude, but he knew if he got too close—it was hell sleeping in the same bed every night as it was—that he'd do something he'd regret. So he spent more time out in the paddocks than he needed to, as well as planting another three huge paddocks of wheat. The last cattle sale paid a huge part of the bank loan back. Five months down, seven to go until the farm was really in the black and most of the loan would be paid off. At worst.

Or should that be at best?

It was going to be difficult when she left for the kids, and if he was honest, for him, too. He'd gotten used to having a wife in the house.

Ned touched the railing at the side of the steps as he walked up to the verandah. He'd come back to the house to get a phone number, and although Jemima had packed his smoko to have in the paddock, he'd arrived back at the house in time for morning tea. He hoped it didn't bother her. Since he'd pulled back, she had been a lot quieter with him, too, and he was sure he could see hurt in her eyes, although it was probably his imagination.

As he stepped onto the verandah, loud rock and roll music blared from the house. It was Tuesday, and Jemima was obviously taking advantage of being alone. Ned frowned. He knew nothing about her background apart from that silly article that had been in the paper a few months back and the fact that she wanted to be a school teacher. Liam and Lucy were protective of her, and the few times he'd asked either of them a question about Jemima, the answer had always been very general.

Family loyalty. He liked it.

Ned didn't even know what sort of music she liked, but he'd assumed it would be something more mellow than the loud music that was belting from the kitchen. He pushed open the wooden screen door and called out, but the music was too loud for anyone to hear him. He crossed the living room, and when he reached the kitchen doorway, a grin spread across his face.

Well, that was another use for a carrot.

Jemima was sashaying along the sink, hips swinging from side to side, hair flying wild, and singing at the top of her voice to a carrot microphone to that *Hippy, Hippy Shake* song. The kitchen was warm and cosy, much warmer than the cool early winter day outside. The kitchen bench was covered with saucepans and vegetables and dusted with flour, and an acrid burning smell filled the kitchen.

Ned was transfixed. Jemima's shorts barely reached the top of her thigh—those gloriously long legs that he'd noticed the first day he'd seen her in that sexy red suit were exposed, and her snug

T-shirt moulded her high breasts. A pair of black square glasses framed her eyes.

God, she was one of the sexiest sights he'd ever seen.

And she was in his kitchen, in his house. He swallowed, unable to take a step forward or back. He was invading her privacy, and he knew she would be embarrassed if she saw him watching.

But he couldn't take his eyes away. The music ended, and she threw the carrot into the sink with a final fancy twirl, her hair flying around her head. She turned and stopped dead when she met Ned's eyes.

Jemima's hand went to her mouth, and he watched as her neck turned red, and then her cheeks flared with heat. And then, surprisingly, her lips lifted, and she let out a deep belly laugh. She threw her head back and held her stomach. Ned tried to keep his eyes on her face, but it took all his willpower.

Finally, she drew a deep breath and sat on the stool at the counter. 'Whoops, sprung!'

He shook his head, though he was still grinning. 'Where's Jemima McCormack gone?'

Her eyes widened, and he realised it was the first time she'd heard those two words together.

'Um, she was cooking'—she picked up a recipe book and pulled a face—' or rather, she was trying to cook, and it wasn't a success, so she needed to work off her frustration. Sorry.'

Ned shook his head. 'There's no need to be sorry. I don't think you've had much fun lately. It was good to see you . . . er . . . letting go.' He chuckled. 'I particularly liked the orange microphone.'

'Well, I didn't need it for the casserole. I burned the meat before I even added the vegetables.' She swept a hand over the countertop, gesturing to neatly chopped piles of carrot, potato, and onion. 'I'm sorry, Ned. It appears I can chop, but cooking is not one of my strengths. Anyway, what are you doing in so early? Did you forget your smoko?'

'No, I needed a phone number, so I thought I'd come in and have a cuppa with you. Is that okay?'

'Of course, it's okay. I'll boil the jug. And there's some of Lucy's fruit cake in the pantry.'

'No pineapple in it?' he asked with a grin.

'No, but I asked her that, too.' Jemima smiled at him, and that devilish ping of desire took off again.

No. Be strong.

He watched as she stood, crossed to the sink, and filled the jug. This time, he let his gaze linger on her long, bare legs.

Shit. The way his thoughts were heading, this would be the last time he'd come to the house when Ryan was at preschool. The direction of his thoughts was entirely inappropriate.

By the time she turned around, he was sitting at the table

and had pulled his phone out, trying to focus on something else. He needed to get these bloody thoughts out of his head.

Not again. And they would be decidedly unwanted from her point of view, he was sure. But Ned certainly wasn't going to stand up in his tight moleskins. Not the way things currently were.

He frowned over the phone. 'Jem, could you please pass me that card with the phone number on the fridge?'

Jemima lifted the fridge magnet that was holding the card in place and walked across to him. Her hair brushed his face, and a waft of her musky body lotion surrounded him. She leaned forward and put the card on the table next to his phone.

Double shit. Get your mind back on the farm.

'Tea or coffee?'

'Um. Coffee, please.' He frowned as he stared at the business card on the table.

'Is everything okay?'

'Yes, fine.' He lifted his head and kept his eyes on her face. 'In fact, things are really great. The back paddocks are looking great, and the cattle are healthy. The wheat's come up, and it's looking green already.' He looked around and gestured to the house. 'You've done an amazing job getting the house in order, and the kids are happy. So, it's more than fine. Yes. Good. Yes. We're on track. Well on track.'

'I'm happy to hear that. I'll get the cake.' She looked at him curiously as she poured the hot water onto the instant coffee and then headed for the pantry again.

Oh, God. This time, he didn't look at her legs and kept his eyes on the phone.

'Do you mind if I clean up the kitchen while you have your coffee? Or do you want company?' After she put the cake tin on the table, she stood beside the countertop and blew on her cup of coffee. 'I'm going to have to thaw some more meat and start from scratch.'

The last thing Ned wanted was Jemima walking around while he was sitting there, trying to get his feelings under control. It was like being an adolescent again. But then, how many farmers had to deal with a world-famous model in a pair of shorts and a tight T-shirt dancing in their kitchen?

'No. Sit down with me. I could do with the company.' Ned lifted his gaze to meet hers. 'We haven't talked much lately. Not since—'

Jemima frowned as she pulled out the chair and put her cup on the table next to the cake. 'No, you've been a bit distant.'

He held her stare. 'I'm sorry. I've had a lot on my mind.'

'I'll make something different for dinner. I thought I'd nailed it with those last couple of lessons, but that damn stove beats me every time.' She changed the subject, and he wondered why she didn't want to talk about . . . about them. Although the last thing that he wanted Jemima to know was that his feelings for her were becoming more than they should be. Much more than a business agreement. It was only the close proximity and the fact that they'd slept together a couple of weeks ago. That was it.

'I've got a better idea,' he said. 'I have to go into town later. Let's pack a change of clothes for the kids and go to the RSL for dinner. It's about time you had a break from the kitchen—and the stove.' He couldn't help himself. He reached over and let himself touch her hand and ignored the little nerve endings that fired in his fingers and sent warmth running up his arm. 'Ryan's sure to be filthy when we pick him up, and the girls won't want to go out in their school uniforms. We could have dinner as soon as the club opens the bistro and still be home before it gets too cold. I'll light the fire before we go, and the house will be warm when we get home.' The more he talked, the less he thought about her standing so close to him.

Jemima shrugged. 'It's up to you. I don't mind cooking.'

He caught her eye and chuckled. 'Really?'

She laughed with him. 'Okay. You caught me out. I don't hate it, but I'm hopeless. How come I can plan a whole lesson plan, write a five-thousand-word essay, and get top marks, but I can't even follow a simple recipe?'

'I guess you can't be good at everything. Cath was a great cook, but the house and garden were always a mess.' As the words left his tongue, Ned pulled himself up. It was the first time he'd ever talked about Cath, and it had come out naturally and without that usual spike of grief. It was good to mention Cath without the awkwardness and sadness. He probed it like a tongue touches gently on a sore tooth.

'I always looked after the washing and the vacuuming because she worked, too, so when it ended up being just me and the kids, I coped a bit easier than some others would have.' No heavy feeling in his chest for a change, and he smiled. 'You've done an amazing job of the front garden and the veggie garden. I don't think I've told you how much I appreciate the extras you've done around here.'

There was a long, loaded silence. She, too, was obviously remembering the "extra" of a few weeks ago, and Ned's thoughts sprang straight back to that glorious night.

'Um.' Jemima cleared her throat. 'What did she do?'

'Cath was in travel. And when Ryan was born, a part-time job came up at the agency in the shopping centre not far from our house. She loved getting out of the house because she wasn't exactly what you'd call a domestic goddess.'

'That makes me feel a bit better,' Jemima said ruefully. 'Domestic goddess, I'll never be.'

Ned's eyes lingered. Maybe not the domestic, but to him, Jemima looked like a goddess, no matter what she was wearing or doing.

He lowered his eyes and stared down at the coffee cup. 'So don't ever worry that you're letting us down. You're doing great, and I appreciate it very much. You've been so good with the kids. And the house.' He needed to bring the conversation and his thoughts back to the agreement. It was altogether too intimate in the kitchen together, especially with her in those shorts and snug T-shirt.

'And besides, I didn't ask you to help out with your cooking skills. I got the loan, and things are going well. The loan's coming down much quicker than I'd hoped. Cattle prices are really good.'

He drained his cup and stood. It was safe now. 'I've got to go to my office and call the supplier. I might need the spreadsheet.'

He crossed to the door and turned around. Jemima had a strange look on her face. 'So, if you can pack a change of clothes for the kids and get yourself glammed up, we'll head into town about two. Does that suit?'

She nodded, but her voice was quiet. 'That's fine.'

Chapter Nineteen

While she ate her sandwich for lunch, Jemima stood on the verandah and stared over the wheat paddocks. The second batch of meat was browning on the stove. She'd pulled another lot of steak from the freezer—at least she knew the right way to thaw it now. It was a shame to waste the chopped vegetables, so she was going to put a casserole in the slow cooker and have it ready for tomorrow night.

Jemima smiled. She had a better handle on this cooking now. She'd always wondered what a slow cooker was, and now she knew how to use one. Ned had gone back out to the paddocks after he made his call, but he hadn't come back in for his lunch, so she assumed he'd substitute his smoko for a lunch break.

She was pleased to have the space. Every time she thought about him seeing her dancing and singing in the kitchen that morning, prickly heat ran down her back. The music and the silly dancing had eased her frustration when she'd burned the meat.

And not only frustration with my cooking skills. All she thought about was Ned; all she wanted to do was be held by him. Get close to him and inhale that gorgeous manly smell. Feel the whipcord strength of his muscles on his arms. Lean against that washboard stomach and run her fingers…

Enough.

But ever since the night they'd given in and had sex, he'd kept her at a distance. She even swore that he'd added another pillow to that stupid pillow fence between them. Until he'd talked to her today—and surprisingly mentioned his wife—they'd barely had a conversation apart from anything to do with the children or a simple 'please pass the salt.' So she needed to forget all her stupid fantasies.

But when she'd turned around and met Ned's laughing eyes, she would swear she'd seen a spark of desire in his gaze.

It had been so hard to look away as he'd stared. Frustration had slammed through her. She had to remember Ned thought of her as a business solution. And like everyone else, he obviously didn't see past her looks or these stupid shorts she'd put on that morning.

Maybe she should go to town and go on a date. Jemima grabbed the railing and shook her head.

Stupid. For a minute, she'd forgotten that, as far as everyone was concerned, she was a married woman and stepmother. She couldn't go on a date, although a smile crept over her face, imagining what the Sykes' gossip mill would do if she went out on the town. A giggle bubbled up in her chest—about the only chance to "go out on the town" in Prickle Creek was to go to the ballroom dancing lessons at the RSL. Lucy had enticed her there not long after she'd arrived back home. They'd left quickly. They'd been the only ones in the hall under eighty. And besides, any night out and any hint of gossip about her would be the end of a chance to get a job at the local school.

As she turned back to the house, Jemima wondered what it would be like to dance with Ned. She'd never know. More and more, she was coming to the decision that when her year was up, she'd move back to Sydney to get a teaching job. Or maybe to a larger regional school—that would be better.

As far away from Ned as she could get.

Get your mind back in the kitchen. Forget Ned McCormack. She was going to have to get used to not being here soon. Jemima sniffed.

What was that burning smell?

God, the recipe had said to coat the meat in flour and then brown it, so she assumed it would need a high heat. As she raced back in, the smoke alarm set up its strident screech, and she picked up the tea towel and flicked it until it stopped.

She grabbed the pan and lifted the second ruined lot of meat from the stove.

Tears pricked at her eyes as she tipped the second blackened mess into the pig bucket and then soaked the pan.

Jemima sat at the table and put her hand on her folded arms.

For a minute, she wondered if she'd be better off back in the modelling world.

***

Ned whistled to the dogs and secured them in their run before he walked across to the house. He'd left the ute down at the paddock because it was still loaded with irrigation pipes he'd need tomorrow. He was setting up a watering system in the paddock behind the house, ready to plant the next wheat. There were some cattle weights to be entered into this spreadsheet before he had his shower, and they went into town. He was looking forward to going out to the club for dinner.

Be honest.

He was looking forward to coming into the house early and spending some more time with Jemima without the kids around. Taking off his boots, he threw them on the verandah and opened the screen door—he'd oiled it, and the usual squeak was gone. Padding on the tiled floor, his socks made no noise. The music had stopped, but the acrid burning smell lingered. He frowned as he reached the kitchen; Jemima was sitting at the table with her head on her arms on the tabletop.

He hurried across, and she lifted her head. He crouched beside her.

'Jemmy, what's wrong?'

Her cheeks were streaked with tears, and as she stared at

him, her cheeks reddened.

'Oh, nothing, just another burned lot of meat. At the rate I'm going, you'll need to take out another loan to pay for the meat I've ruined.' She sat up straight. 'It's okay. Ignore me. I'm just having a female hormonal moment. You'll need to get used to them with two daughters growing up.' She smiled as she pushed the chair back. 'I'll get you a sandwich.'

He reached out and took her arm before she could move away. 'No, it's fine. I'm not hungry.'

Not for food, anyway. All he wanted to do was hold her. He was a sucker for tears. Ned let go of her arm and looked at the mess in the sink. 'How about I help you clean up this mess?'

'There's no need. You've got stuff to do.'

'No, I'll help. Where's the pot scrubber?'

Ned washed and scrubbed pots while Jemima wiped the dishes and put them away. It was a cosy domestic scene, and he was conscious that they were home alone.

Keep your mind on the task at hand.

'Ned, do you mind if I ask you something?' Jemima's voice was soft.

'No. What's up?'

'How did Cath die?' She hurried on. 'I wouldn't have asked, but you mentioned her easily before. You rarely speak of her, but the kids often do when you're not around, and I didn't want to say the wrong thing. Was she sick?'

Ned put the pot scrubber on the side of the sink and turned to look at her. Jemmy was biting her lip, a surefire sign that she was nervous. He'd gotten to know that sign very well. He stared at her lips. Her face was beautiful, even though her eyes were a little puffy from her tears.

He reached up and ran his thumb gently beneath her eye, where the traces of a tear remained. She drew a quick breath.

'No. She wasn't sick. She was on her way to work. I was working from home and looking after Ryan and Gwennie. A guy went through a stop sign and straight into the side of her car.' Ned kept his tone even. It was the first time, for a long time, he'd talked about it. 'Cath was in hospital on life support for a long time before we…before she died.'

Another tear plopped onto his finger, and he caught it. 'That's what wiped me out financially. I can talk about it now. And I really do need to start talking about Cath naturally to the kids.'

Jemima sniffed and reached for a tissue. 'I think that would be good.'

'Don't cry.'

'It's not that.' She shook her head. 'My mum died in a car accident when I was in my teens. And her two sisters, too. Lucy's mum, and Seb's mum. I know what an impact that had on our family, but we had each other.' Another sniff. 'It breaks my heart that you did it pretty much alone with the kids.'

'My parents and Cath's were great, but all I wanted was to be alone. Coming out here has been so much better than I thought. We've moved on a lot faster than I thought we would.'

Another tear trickled down Jemmy's cheek, and Ned held his arms out. 'A hug would help us both now, I think.' He held her close and murmured into her hair. 'I'm sorry to hear about your family tragedy. We get so tied up in our own grief that it's easy to forget that others have had hard times, too.'

'We're fine now. Unlike your kids, Liam and I didn't have a dad to turn to. Dad died when Liam and I were both small.' Jemima's breath was warm against his cheek.

Ned couldn't help himself. He moved his head closer so her lips were against his cheek. With a sigh, she pressed them against his skin. Ned moved away and lifted his hand. He held her chin gently in his fingers and looked into her blue eyes.

'You are so beautiful, Jemmy. I'm sorry; I didn't mean for this to happen.'

He knew it was okay when she lifted her lips to his.

***

Jemima stood beneath the shower an hour later. They'd left the kitchen spick and span and headed for the bedroom. She'd laughed as Ned had chucked the pillows on the floor and pulled her down beside him. There'd been no more words until they'd realised they only had half an hour to shower and get into town before school finished.

As they drove into town, she tried to block Ned's words from her head. All he'd said was that she was beautiful. Her dreams of being held by him—and more, much more—had come true. But it was only because of her looks.

How many times had that happened in her life? Sometimes, she wished she'd been born a plain Jane. Life would be a lot easier.

'Penny for your thoughts?' His words intruded into her musing.

Jemima forced a smile to her face. 'I was just wondering how you liked driving my car instead of the old ute.'

'It's very nice.'

'Maybe I should sell it to you when I leave. The kids like it.'

'Out of my budget,' he said with a laugh.

'Ned, I've been thinking about when I leave. We need to talk about it. I've had an idea.'

'Yes?' It was hard to tell what he was thinking. Jemima glanced across at him, but he was staring at the road ahead. They were almost in town.

'What do you think if I go away a bit now and then? I can say I've got things to do in Sydney. The kids will get used to me not being there, and it won't be so hard when I go for good in a few months.'

'No. I don't think I could cope with that. Even though Billy's here, I'm still out on the farm a lot.' This time, his words were clipped. 'And it would cause talk that would get back to the kids.'

'You don't think me going at the end of the year will cause more talk and do them even more harm? We really didn't think this through, Ned.' The anger was welcome, and Jemima stopped feeling sorry for herself. 'And me not cuddling and being affectionate with the kids? Kelsey almost broke my heart at Pony Club last week. She came running up for a hug when she did well. When I stepped back and patted her shoulder, the look on her face almost broke my heart.'

'So, what do you suggest? You go back to cuddling the kids, and then you leave for a few weeks at a time? You think that won't hurt them?'

'Ned, you're not getting it. Whatever I do, they've gotten really used to having me around. It's going to hurt them no matter what.'

Ned's knuckles were white as they gripped the steering wheel of her Audi. 'I know. Just let me think on it some more. I'll give it some more thought, and we'll talk when we get home. Okay?'

His eyes were shadowed as he parked the car across from

the school. 'You stay here. I'll go and collect them. Might as well start now.'

Jemima pulled out her phone and scrolled through the numbers until she found Angie's work number. She hit the dial button and waited for Angie to pick up.

'Hi Ange. It's Jemmy. Can I ask a favour?'

Chapter Twenty

The RSL bistro was busy, humming with the noise of the end of week crowd. The Friday night raffles were on, and the kids were fascinated as the winning numbers flashed up on the screen. Several families from the primary school were there, and Kelsey, Gwennie, and Ryan had joined their friends sliding up and down the polished timber floor next to where the carpet bowls were played. When Jemima asked Angie about the kids having a shower and a change of clothes at her little house in town, Angie asked if she and Liam could join them for dinner, too.

Liam and Ned were deep in conversation about cattle as they waited for their meals to be called. Two men in Salvation Army uniforms were moving from table to table collecting money. After Angie and Jemima had slipped some coins into the wooden box, Angie leaned over.

'You okay, Jemmy? You're very quiet tonight, and your eyes are shadowed.'

Jemima nodded and then let out a sigh. 'Not really. I've got a bit on my mind. And I've been really tired.'

'Being a surrogate mum and a housekeeper taking its toll?' Angie said with a smile.

'Not really. The cooking's the only thing that I can't handle. But I'm getting better at it. I've been tired and off-colour ever since Lucy tried to poison us all with her pineapple pizza!'

'She still feels so bad about that.'

'You were lucky you were away that weekend. It wasn't fun.'

'But Lucy said Ned looked after you okay?'

'He did.' Jemima couldn't help the colour that ran into her cheeks.

'He's a good man. And he's good with those kids.' Angie dropped her voice. 'Lucy and I were hoping—'

'Don't go hoping anything. It ain't gonna happen.' Jemima held up her hand. 'Purely business, and it's coming to an end. Maybe sooner rather than later. We're talking about an exit strategy at the moment. The farm's going really well.'

'Oh no. An exit strategy? What are you going to do?' Angie asked with a frown.

'Find a school job somewhere.'

'I'll miss you—we'll all miss you if you move away, but, hey, Did Liam tell you the news yet?'

'No, what news?' Jemima scrunched her nose up.

'Your cousin Seb is coming home.'

'No, he didn't tell me!' Jemima glanced over at her brother but he and Ned were still deep in conversation, a serious one by their expressions. 'When?'

'Next week. He's stuff to do in Sydney, and then he'll ride his bike up.'

'I can't wait to see him.' Jemima smiled—something to keep her mind off her dilemma.

They were interrupted by the buzzer on the table calling them to collect their meals.

'I'll go and round up the kids,' Jemima said.

'No. I'll go.'

Liam looked at Ned curiously as he stood and left the table.

'Everything okay with you two?' he asked. 'You've barely exchanged a word since we got here.'

'Yep. Just fine and dandy.' Jemima forced a smile to her face as she pushed her chair back. 'Come and help me get a tray and load these meals up.'

It was strange being isolated from the kids by Ned's actions tonight. If that was his new strategy for preparing them for her departure, she didn't think much of it and she would tell him that the first opportunity she got.

Or maybe she wouldn't.

Things came to a head much more quickly than she'd anticipated. As the children were eating their ice cream, Ned leaned over to Liam.

'Can you keep an eye on the kids for a minute? I want to

talk to Jemima about something.'

He stood and pulled her chair out for her and beckoned her to follow him to the doors that led to the balcony overlooking the car park.

Ned held the door open for her.

When they were outside, he stepped away and leaned against the railing.

'What's wrong? What couldn't wait till we got home?' she asked.

'I've been thinking about what you said. And I'm sorry I argued. You're absolutely right. The longer you stay, the worse it's going to be for the kids.' He folded his arms. 'Liam told me Seb's coming home soon. It's a perfect excuse.'

'Excuse?'

'You can drop us home and then go straight over to Prickle Creek Farm. I'll tell the kids your cousin is coming to visit, and you're really excited about seeing him.'

'I am,' she said, and if there was a bit of snarkiness in her tone, she didn't mind. 'But he's not arriving till next week.'

'Oh.' He frowned.

Tonight? Ned wants to give me the flick tonight? Snark was good; it helped deal with the hurt. She'd been right all along— well, ever since the night the pillow fence had gone down. Ned didn't care about her. She was the only fool who had fallen in love.

Yes, she admitted it to herself. Not only had she fallen for his three beautiful children, she'd fallen for him, too.

Jemima drew a deep breath, and the sharp ache that pierced her chest was the way a heart must feel when it was breaking. 'Excellent.' She folded her arms against her aching chest. 'I'm pleased that you've seen what's best for them. They don't have to know that he's not coming for a few days. I'll just keep a low profile.' She couldn't believe it. When she'd suggested going to Sydney now and then, Ned had said he couldn't manage on the farm with only Billy.

'Yes. It will be for the best. It will be tough to start with, but they'll be fine.'

'So, is this it? Just for a while for them to get used to it, or do you want me to leave for good now?'

'Maybe,' he said slowly. 'Maybe it would be better if we do it in one swoop. You can stay over at Prickle Creek because Seb's visiting and the kids will get used to it.'

'You think?'

'No, I don't think that.' Ned's expression was bleak, and his tone was harsh. 'I owe you so much for helping out when I needed it, but it's the best way.'

'So how are you going to cope on the farm? And look after the kids?' She knew her voice was tight, but she didn't give a damn.

'Liam's got onto a bloke who's looking for some part-time farm work. He's coming out to see me tomorrow.'

'Fabulous. You don't need me at all then.'

'Jemmy...don't be—'

'My name is Jemima.' The only way to fight back the hurt that was flooding through her was with anger. 'Right then. I'll drop you home and then go to the farm. And after Sebastian arrives, I'll go back to Sydney for a while. When will you tell the kids?'

'In a few days.'

'And when do you want me to move my stuff out?'

'I'll call you when I've told them, and maybe you can come over and get it Tuesday when they're all at school.'

The reality of her happy-families-playing-Mummy coming to an end hit Jemima like a physical blow. The kids wanted her . . . but Ned? Ned had only needed her for the bank loan and the nannying . . . and, of course, her body.

'If there's any debt incurred at the bank by me leaving early, let me know. I'll settle it for you.'

'That's not necessary.' Ned ran a hand over his face with a sigh. 'Look, Jemmy—I mean Jemima—'

She blinked back tears as she looked over at Ned. 'Can I ask you one thing? Please?'

He nodded.

'Can I hug them good-bye tonight?'

Ned nodded again without speaking. His mouth was set in a straight line.

He opened the door, and they went back into the dining room. The children had finished their ice cream.

Angie raised her eyebrows, and Jemima shook her head. The band started up, and it was too noisy to speak as the music filled the club. She swallowed, forcing back the ache in her throat. A happy family night at the club had turned into her worst nightmare. She wasn't ready for this yet. But she had to be because Ned had decided.

A few elderly couples got up on the dance floor, and Jemima tried to smile as they launched into a gypsy tap. She'd never get to dance with Ned like she'd dreamed about. The ache in her throat was unbearable, and she didn't know how she was going to make the trip home without breaking in front of the kids. He didn't need her anymore.

Ned had sprung this on her too quickly. She wasn't prepared, and she wasn't ready to leave the children. Her heart ached the most for the kids. No matter what their father thought, she knew that Kelsey, Gwennie, and Ryan would miss her. The girls, especially, needed a mother figure in their life. Her breath hitched on a sob. Well, it wasn't going to be her. She wasn't good enough.

Liam pulled Angie up for a dance. Jemima watched as her

brother held his fiancée close when the band changed to a waltz.

Gwennie tugged on her arm. 'Jemmy, will you dance with me? Some of the other kids are up there.'

She looked at Ned and managed to keep her voice level. 'Do we have time before we go home? Ryan's looking sleepy.'

To his credit, Ned smiled and spoke naturally, although he didn't meet Jemima's eyes as he bent down to Gwennie. 'Time for one quick dance.' He looked around. 'Where's Kelsey?'

'Outside with her friends.'

'Okay. I'll go and tell her we're about to go while Jemima dances with you.' He hoisted Ryan onto his hip, and Jemima watched as he walked across to the door until Gwennie tugged her hand.

'Come on. We've learned some dances at school.'

How could such a beautiful afternoon turn sour so quickly?

Jemima smiled, danced, and twirled Gwennie around and even managed a couple of laughs.

'Come on, Daddy will be waiting.' She took Gwennie's hand and passed by the table where Liam and Angie were sitting after their dance. 'I'll see you pair later. I'm going to come over to Prickle Creek after I drop Ned and the kids off at home.'

Liam raised his eyebrows in a frown, and Jemima looked away. She knew her eyes were bright with tears.

'Oh, can I come, too?' Gwennie's smile almost broke her

heart—again. Could a heart break twice in one night?

'Not tonight, sweetie,' she said quietly.

##

Kelsey was extra quiet on the way home, but luckily, Gwennie's chatter about the super night she'd had, the yummy chips and gravy, and the red fire engine drink filled the silence. Ned drove her car, and when he pulled up at the house, Jemima opened the passenger door and climbed out.

'Do you want me to help you get Ryan inside?'

'No. I'm fine, thank you.' Ned opened the back door and lifted Ryan out. Kelsey flung open the other door and ran inside before Jemima could say goodbye.

'Good night, Jemmy.' Gwennie took her hand as she helped the little girl out of the back seat. With a pleading glance at Ned, Jemima crouched down and put her arms around the little girl. 'Bye-bye, darling. You be good for Daddy, won't you?'

'I will. See you tomorrow. Remember you promised we could make fairy cakes like they learned you at your CWA school.'

'Taught, not learned.' Ned held Ryan on his shoulder, held out his other hand to Gwennie, and lowered his voice. 'Good night, Jemmy. I'll call you.'

She bit her lip and nodded as Gwennie piped up. 'Daddy. You forgot to kiss Mummy . . . I mean Jemmy . . . good night.'

'So I did.'

Jemima stood still as he leaned over and brushed her mouth with firm, cool lips. 'Goodbye,' he said, and she would swear till her dying day that Ned's voice broke.

She held it together until she drove out of the gate and across the road to Prickle Creek Farm.

Chapter Twenty-One

Ned tucked the kids into bed and gave each of them an extra cuddle in an attempt to make himself feel like less of a louse. Rather than draw it out, he'd tell them tomorrow morning what was happening so they had time to get used to the idea before the girls went back to school on Monday. He would take Ryan out in the ute in the morning, and then Billy and the new guy could work with the cattle in the afternoon while Ryan had his sleep and he got dinner ready. Tuesday was preschool day, so he could get the house in order and—

Ned shook his head as he walked down the hallway, feeling lost. *What the bloody hell have I done?*

Everywhere he looked, he could see Jemima. Playing hide-and-seek with Ryan, sitting at the desk helping Gwennie with her reading. Looking at horse magazines with Kelsey. He paused at the door to their—*his*—bedroom. All he could see was Jemima lying there, smiling at him as he'd dismantled that bloody wall of pillows that afternoon.

He'd done the only thing he could, and he'd done it at the right time. It was time to let her go before he fell in love with her.

He'd seen the look in Jemmy's eyes when she'd said

goodbye to Gwennie, and her body had been stiff and straight when he'd brushed her lips. She was a good person, and he would be grateful to her for the rest of his life for teaching him how important the whole affection thing was. He hadn't been fair to her. He'd used her to get the bank loan that let him have more time to spend with the kids, and he'd taken her to his bed. He'd never intended for her to become a part of the family. And after the first time he'd slept with her, he'd vowed to remain aloof and not be tempted again, but…

He wandered into the kitchen, feeling lost, knowing Jemima wasn't going to be in there. A reluctant smile tugged at his lips; a smell of burnt pots still lingered even though he had scrubbed them clean. Was it only this afternoon that they'd ended up in his bed?

Whoever would have thought that an international fashion model would have come into their lives and made such a difference? It was just like that movie with Goldie Hawn—what was it called? *Overboard*, that was it. Jemima was beautiful enough to have starred in it herself.

She'd been wonderful with the kids, and he knew that she would make a wonderful stepmother. *A real one.*

But that wasn't going to happen because he wasn't going to risk falling in love again. It had been so bloody horrendous when he'd lost Cath; he honestly couldn't go through that again. And he wouldn't put the kids at that risk again. Ned stared through the window, ignoring the little voice that was telling him it was already too late. He loved Jemima already. He straightened his shoulders and took a deep breath.

Yes, this is the best way. The only way.

He was so close to needing Jemmy in his life that it was time to end it.

Why was he such a coward? What the heck had he been thinking, taking her to bed when he didn't have the courage to make it permanent? On the flip side, how was he going to live without her?

He couldn't afford to trust what his heart was telling him.

Go after her. Tell her you love her.

In came the logical mind.

No, we can live without her. What if she had an accident? Life is fragile.

And how did he even know that Jemmy loved him back?

Of course she does, his heart told him.

What if she thinks I only wanted her for her money? In came those thoughts again.

Ned looked around the kitchen. His eyes went back to the window. It was pitch dark outside, and that was what his life—and the children's lives—would be like if he let her go.

At that moment, his heart won. He looked up at the clock

above the door. It was only nine o'clock. The kids could sleep in tomorrow.

They were all going to Prickle Creek Farm. He was going to ask Jemima Smythe to marry him.

For real, this time.

***

There was a tap on Jemima's bedroom door. She wiped her eyes and shoved the tissue beneath the pillow. 'Yes?'

'Are you decent?' Liam called through the door.

'Yes, what's up?'

The door opened, and Liam poked his head around it.

'You okay?' Liam flicked the light switch on, and Jemima put her hands over her eyes.

'Yes. Just a bit emotional.'

'Why? What's going on?'

Jemima sat up and tucked her legs beneath her on the bed as Liam sat on the end. The house phone rang, and Angie yelled out, 'I've got it.'

'Have you been crying?' Liam looked at her curiously.

'Yeah,' she sniffed. 'I've been so bloody emotional lately it'll be good to get back to my apartment and put an end to the nonstop waterworks.'

'Whoa, right there. What do you mean back to your apartment?'

'Ned and I both agreed it's best for the kids to put an end to this farce now. The farm's doing really well, and he's going to pay the loan back. And he's hired that other farmhand, so there's no need for me to hang around.'

Liam shook his head slowly. 'And what about the fact that you're in love with each other.'

'No, we're not. Don't be stupid.'

'I'm not blind, Jemmy. You should see the way he looks at you.'

Her voice was cold and cynical. 'That's nothing new. I have hundreds of people looking at me like that every time I get on the catwalk. Besides, he told me I was beautiful, but he didn't tell me that he loved me.' The words wobbled, and she dug under the pillow for the tissue as her eyes welled up. 'Bloody tears. Why won't they stop?'

'Don't you dare make the same mistake that Angie and I did? Go and talk to Ned. Make sure he knows how you feel. Please promise me you'll do that before you go anywhere?'

'Maybe.'

'Jemima.'

'Oh, maybe. All right. I'll think about it.'

They both jumped as Angie pushed the door open. Her eyes were wide, and her face was pale. 'We need to go over to Ned's. Now.'

Jemima jumped to her feet. 'What's wrong?'

'Kelsey's missing.' The look she shot at Jemima was sympathetic.

'Oh no. How can she be missing?' Jemima pulled on her sweatshirt and grabbed her car keys from the dressing table.

'Ned said he was on his way to bed and checked on the kids and she was gone. He's searched everywhere. The house, the hay shed, and he's about to load the other two kids in the ute and head down to the dams.' Angie looked at Liam as Jemima pulled the door wide open. 'He asked if you'd drive along the road and then to the main road. Wait, Jemmy. I'll come with you. I told Ned to wait, and I'd sit with Ryan and Gwennie.'

Liam followed them up the hall. 'I'll take my ute up the road.' He gave Angie a quick kiss and picked up his keys. 'I'll see you both over there.'

As Jemima drove to the Prickle Creek Farm gate, she and Angie both kept their eyes peeled for Kelsey, but all they saw were kangaroos, standing sentinel-like next to the trees lit in a ghoulish glow by the headlights on high beam.

Jemima muttered, 'I thought she seemed a bit quiet when we left the club. And when we got home, she ran straight inside.'

'She can't have gotten far in such a short time,' Angie reassured her.

'What if she'd got as far as the main road and hitched a ride with a truckie?'

'She knows better than that, Jemmy.'

Jemima shook her head. 'I just hope she didn't overhear us when we were talking about me leaving. Oh, God, I hope she's all right.'

They cruised along the driveway down to the Daniela homestead but didn't see anyone until the lights settled on Ned standing beside the hay shed.

Jemima pulled the handbrake on, jumped out of the Audi and ran over to him.

'Ned, tell us where you want us to look.' Her heart went out to him, but she pulled her hand back as she went to comfort him.

Ned glanced over at Angie. 'The kids are inside, and Gwennie's really upset.'

'Come on, I'll come down the back with you.' Jemima hurried over to the ute before he had a chance to tell her otherwise.

***

The front yard was filled with a dozen or more utes as neighbours from along the road arrived to join in the search. Jim Ison announced at midnight that the police were on their way out, and the volunteer SES guys were bringing searchlights. Jemima stayed by Ned's side as they searched the back paddocks and roads, but there was no sign of Kelsey. The only hopeful sign was that one of the farm dogs, a young pup, was missing, too, and as they searched, Ned called out for Rusty every few minutes. But there was no answering dog bark and no child to be heard or seen.

By three a.m., the SES was searching the paddocks along the road, and the contract shooters had their spotlighted utes scouring the back paddocks. Jemima grabbed Ned's arm as they finished the circumnavigation of the last wheat paddock.

'Come on. We'll go back to the house and have a break. You can't go on like this all night.'

He shook his head. 'I'm not stopping until I find her.'

Jemima knew the voice of reason would win out. He'd kept in touch with Angie back at the house every fifteen minutes.

'It will be the most logical way. There's a coordinated search being set up.'

Finally, he agreed, and they headed back to the front of the farm. It was lit up with spotlights, and Ned shook his head when he saw how many utes were there. A tented stand had been set up at the back of the house on the lawn, and tears pricked Jemima's eyes. There were at least a dozen women there, making cups of tea and handing out sandwiches. Her eyes widened as she spotted the three Mrs Sykes, all helping out.

The heart of the country, she thought—the people who live on the farms and in the towns. There was nothing like it, and they all pitched in when one of their own was in need.

Ned slumped in the front of the ute and put his hand over

his eyes. 'Where now? Where will we look next?'

'Did you search the house in case she was hiding?'

'I did.'

'Come, and we'll get a cup of tea and then meet with the sergeant.' The white police Pajero with the blue numbers on the top and hood was parked at the gate.

As they walked across to the house, Jemima stopped dead. She put her hand on Ned's arm. 'Ned, wait. Look!'

A little red kelpie wiggled out from under the hay shed wall, covered in straw.

'It's Rusty.' Ned scooped the pup into his arms and ran back to the shed with Jemima close behind him. 'Where is she, Rusty? Take me to her.'

The small dog ran to the stack of hay bales in the corner at the back of the shed and disappeared behind them. Ned called him, and he came from behind them, covered in loose straw again.

'Wait here with Rusty.' Ned picked him up and handed him to Jemima before he walked across to the bales and pushed himself between them and the shed.

'Oh, Kelsey.' Ned's voice shook.

'Daddy,' came the plaintive cry from the back of the hay bales.

As they walked around the front of the shed, Jemima's heart clenched. Kelsey was covered in sticks of straw, and she rubbed her red-rimmed eyes.

'I only went in there so you wouldn't hear me crying, and when Rusty crawled in with me, I went to sleep.' She looked at Jemima, and her lips trembled. 'Don't you love us anymore? Are you sick of us? Are you going to leave us, too? I thought you were going to be my mum, but I don't want you to leave us like Mummy did. I want you to love us all forever.' The last words hitched on a sob.

'There's no need to cry, sweetheart.' Jemima walked over and put her arms around Kelsey.

'There is! I heard Daddy say you were leaving. Please don't leave us. Even if Daddy doesn't want you, we do.' Jemima's heart broke as Kelsey buried her face on her shoulder and started to cry in earnest. 'We love you, Jemmy. Can't you love us back?'

'Oh, sweetheart, I do love you.' Tears filled Jemima's eyes. *What have we done?*

'Kelsey, wait.' Ned's voice was firm. 'I need to tell Jemmy something.'

Jemima looked across at Ned as Kelsey held onto her as though she'd never let go. His eyes held hers, and she waited to hear what he would say.

'Jemima, I made a huge mistake tonight. We *all* want you to be with us. As a mother *and* a wife.'

In a tiny place in her heart, Jemima let the joy of his words take root, but she shook her head. She needed more than that; she didn't need to be wanted for how useful she was, no matter how much the kids loved her.

'Why?' She kept her voice soft. 'Why do you want me to stay?' Her eyes challenged Ned's as she dug deep for the strength to resist Kelsey's plea.

Ned reached out and moved Kelsey gently away from Jemima. She frowned as he got down onto one knee. It was strange looking down at him. Kelsey stood beside her father with one hand on his shoulder and a broad smile on her lips as Ned took Jemima's hand and pressed his lips to her palm.

'I want you to stay because I love you.'

Joy spiralled through her as she saw the honesty and love in his eyes.

'I was wrong to tell you to go. I was crazy. I couldn't bear the thought of losing you, but by sending you away, that's what I was doing. Losing you. I *love* you, Jemmy. I always will.'

Jemima looked down at the tanned and strong hand holding hers, and her heart flooded with all the love she'd been holding back.

Kelsey took her other hand. 'Can you love Daddy back? He's very nice, really he is.'

'I know that already, darling.' Jemima tugged on Ned's hand, and he stood up beside her. 'And yes, I do love your daddy.'

She held Ned's beautiful brown eyes as she answered. 'Would you mind if he kissed me?'

Kelsey shook her head and smiled. Ned lowered his head, and his lips took Jemima's in the sweetest kiss. A soft kiss she would remember for the rest of her life.

A kiss full of love. A kiss full of promise.

'Does that mean you're going to stay forever?' Kelsey's voice interrupted them, and Ned pulled away with a chuckle.

'No one can promise forever, sweetie.' Jemima looked up and held Ned's eyes with hers. 'But as long as humanly possible, I promise I will love you, all of you, and stay with you, and Gwennie and Ryan . . . and your Daddy, if you *all* want me to.'

Ned's eyes gave his answer, and Kelsey cried out, 'Oh yes, Jemmy. We all want you to. We love you.'

'We'd better go out and tell everyone that you've been found, young lady.' Ned put his arms out and lifted Kelsey up while Jemima carried the pup.

The cheers that resounded around the paddocks that night would stay with Jemima always. She was home, and she was here to stay.

Epilogue

A month later, Jemima walked out of the doctor's surgery in Prickle Creek. Ned had gone to Cartwright's store, and she'd had an appointment with Dr Wenham. The old doc had been in the surgery since she was a child. Ned had insisted that she have a check-up because she'd been so tired, but Jemima thought it was only because of the different sort of work she'd been doing over the past six months.

She stepped out into the winter sun and pulled her coat around her. The stiff, westerly wind blew straight down the main street, and everyone who was out there scurried into shelter as soon as they could. Wandering slowly down the street, she felt like pinching herself as happiness almost overwhelmed her. Her husband was chatting to Kev Cartwright at the door of the produce store, and his face lit up with a smile as she walked towards them. As she approached, he excused himself and hurried over to her, his smile replaced with a look of concern.

'Are you all right, darling? You look pale. Were the test results okay?' Ned put his arm around her and shielded her from the cold wind as they walked to the ute.

'They were. But Lucy's going to be surprised. We can't blame the pineapple for me not feeling right.'

Ned frowned. 'The pineapple? That was ages ago.'

'Yes, but apparently, when you have a tummy upset, the pill doesn't do what it's supposed to.'

Jemima chuckled as Ned's mouth dropped open. 'If the wind changes, you'll stay like that.' She put her hand beneath his chin and gently pushed his mouth shut.

'You mean you're . . . we're . . .'

'Yep. I hope that's okay. Just as well we're married, isn't it?' Her words were muffled as Ned put his arms around her and kissed her, not caring who was watching them.

'I've got something to say about that,' he said. 'But after we tell the kids. I think this calls for a milkshake at Con's when we pick them up. What do you reckon?'

Jemima rubbed her still-flat stomach. 'I agree. Milk's good for pregnancy, so they tell me.'

***

It was Saturday night, and Ned had sworn Jemima and the kids to secrecy. The pregnancy was to be their family secret just for a few days. As he drove back in through the gate—the special passengers safely in the ute— he was pleased to see that all of the guests had arrived. Liam's ute was parked beside Lucy and Garth's SUV. He'd refused to tell anyone why he was going to Dubbo, just tapping the side of his nose and saying, 'You'll see.'

'*Ssh,*' he whispered to his passengers as they walked behind him to the house.

Jemima was standing with Lucy and Angie. Garth and Liam had fired up the barbeque. She wore those loose pants and a fitted T-shirt, and a surge of pride filled him to think that she was carrying his child. She looked up and caught his eyes, and as she smiled at him, happiness flooded through him.

'Nanny, Grandpa!' Gwennie was the first to spot his parents, but Kelsey and Ryan ran just as fast and reached their grandparents at the same time.

'Oh, what a lovely surprise.' Jemmy's warm breath whispered in his ear, and he put his arm around her.

'That's only half of it. Once the hubbub dies down, we'll see the next bit.' Her beautiful arched eyebrows rose, and she brushed her lips against his. 'I'm sure the children will love whatever you've done.

'I'm sure they will,' he replied with a grin.

Once the greetings had died down and Jemmy had been introduced to his parents, Ned put his fingers in his mouth and whistled. It was the only way he could be heard over the din.

'Come on, you lot. I've got another surprise. Everyone come over here.' He stood on the pavers beside his mother's rose garden. Jemima had done an amazing job of bringing it back to life.

He took her hand and led her to the wrought iron table and

chair set beside the small fountain that was fed by the bore. 'Ryan, Kelsey, Gwennie, I want you here, too.'

He'd told the kids what was going to happen, and Gwennie was under threat of being grounded for life if she talked about it at school.

Ned looked around the families that were gathered around them. The only ones missing were his sister and Jemima's grandparents, but they'd all promised to come for a visit at Christmas.

'Thank you all for being a part of our celebration today. We've got two lots of news, and this is the first one. Ryan?'

Ned dropped to his knee as Ryan pulled a small royal blue box from his pocket with—Ned smiled—a very grubby hand. Kelsey and Gwennie stood beside Ned, a hand on each of his shoulders, and Ryan crouched in front of them.

Together, three loud voices blended with Ned's as he held out a diamond and sapphire ring. 'Jemmy, will you do us the honour of being a wife and mother?'

Ryan continued. 'That's Daddy's wife and our *muvva*, we mean.'

Jemima's beautiful blue eyes were awash with tears as she gazed back at him. 'Yes, I will.' She turned to the three children, 'And that's another yes, yes, and yes!'

'And for the rest of you, there's a yes, number four, too.'

Jemima stood and patted her stomach. 'Our family is growing.'

Sebastian's story is next.
Come and meet Isabella.

Isabella:

eBook:
https://books2read.com/u/310B6w
Print:
https://annieseatonstore.ecwid.com/Isabella-A-Prickle-Creek-Romance-PRE-ORDER-April-p712102293

NOTE:
Previously published in the US as *His Outback Temptation*

Glossary of Aussie terms

Bore: a bore is where you find groundwater that has been accessed by drilling a bore into underground water storages called aquifers.

CWA: (Country Women's Association) The CWA is the largest women's organisation in Australia and aims to improve conditions for country women and children.

Dam: a reservoir used as a water supply.

Derro: Australian slang for a homeless person, a social derelict.

Gumtree: an online classifieds website

Larrikin: a mischievous young person, rowdy and good-hearted, with a sense of humour.

Milk bar: a corner shop that sells milkshakes and other refreshments.

Paddock: small field

Pajero: A type of four-wheel drive vehicle

Prickle: a short-pointed outgrowth on a plant; a small thorn.

Pilliga Scrub: is a forest of some 3,000 square km of semi-arid woodland in temperate north-central New South Wales, Australia.

RSL: The Returned and Services League, Australia (RSL) is a support organisation for men and women who have served or are serving in the Defence Force and provides a social club in communities.

Tuckshop: a school cafeteria

Ute: a utility vehicle; a pick-up in Australia or New Zealand

Also by Annie Seaton

Daughters of the Darling
From Across the Sea
Over the River
By the Billabong (2025)

A Bec Whitfield Mystery
Bowen River
Shadows on the Shore (June 2025)

Duckinwilla Days
Coming Home
Secrets and Surprises
Books 3-7 to follow in 2025

Home to the Outback *(2025)*
Lucy
Angie
Jemima
Isabella

Porter Sisters Series
Kakadu Sunset
Daintree
Diamond Sky
Hidden Valley
Larapinta

JEMIMA

Kakadu Dawn

Others
Whitsunday Dawn
Undara
Osprey Reef
East of Alice
One Summer in Tuscany
Four Seasons Short and Sweet
Follow the Sun
Ten Days in Paradise
Deadly Secrets
Adventures in Time
Silver Valley Witch
The Emerald Necklace
A Clever Christmas
Christmas with the Boss
Her Christmas Star
The Emerald Necklace

The Augathella Girls Series
Outback Roads
Outback Sky
Outback Escape
Outback Wind
Outback Dawn
Outback Moonlight
Outback Dust
Outback Hope
Boxed Sets
Augathella Girls 1-4

JEMIMA

Augathella Girls 5-8

Augathella Short and Sweet Series
An Augathella Surprise
An Augathella Baby
An Augathella Spring
An Augathella Christmas
An Augathella Wedding
An Augathella Easter
An Augathella Masquerade Ball
Boxed Set
Augathella Short and Sweet 1-3
Augathella Short and Sweet 4-7

Sunshine Coast Series
Waiting for Ana
The Trouble with Jack
Healing His Heart
Sunshine Coast **Boxed Set**

The Richards Brothers Series
The Trouble with Paradise
Marry in Haste
Outback Sunrise
Richards Brothers Boxed Set
Bondi Beach Love Series
Beach House
Beach Music
Beach Walk
Beach Dreams
The House on the Hill **Boxed Set**

Second Chance Bay Series

Her Outback Playboy
Her Outback Protector
Her Outback Haven
Her Outback Paradise

Boxed Set

The McDougalls of Second Chance Bay **Boxed Set**

Love Across Time Series

Come Back to Me
Follow Me
Finding Home
The Threads that Bind

Boxed Set

Love Across Time 1-4

Bindarra Creek

Worth the Wait
Full Circle
Secrets of River Cottage
A Clever Christmas
A Place to Belong

About the Author

Annie lives in Australia, on the beautiful north coast of New South Wales. She sits in her writing chair and looks out over the tranquil Pacific Ocean.

She writes contemporary romance and outback crime and loves telling stories that always have a happily ever after. She lives with her very own hero of many years and they share their home with Barney, the rag doll puss, who hides when the four grandchildren come to visit.

Stay up to date with her latest releases at her website: **http://www.annieseaton.net**

If you would like to stay up to date with Annie's releases, subscribe to her newsletter here: http://www.annieseaton.net